BLOOD IN THE DESERT SAND

BLOOD IN THE DESERT SAND

Joe And Kay West novel

LANCE FIGGINS

Primix Publishing
East Brunswick Office Evolution
1 Tower Center Boulevard, Ste 1510
East Brunswick, NJ 08816
www.primixpublishing.com
Phone: 1-800-538-5788

Published by Primix Publishing: 10/24/2024

ISBN: 979-8-89194-327-8(sc)
ISBN: 979-8-89194-328-5(hc)
ISBN: 979-8-89194-329-2(e)

Library of Congress Control Number: 2024918701

CONTENTS

PROLOGUE

Kay slowly moved the crosshairs away from Joe as she scanned the area. With his hands tied behind his back, there was no way he could protect himself.

She knew Hector would kill him if she fired or showed herself. It was only two hundred yards, although Hector was always way too close to Joe, putting Joe continuously in the sight picture. She knew the light bullet could drift just a few inches. In that case, she could or would hit Joe.

Joe yelled, "Kay run!"

Instead of running away, Joe ran at the men charging the camp. With a knife in one hand and his 9MM Glock in the other, he met the charge with deadly force. Dropping to one knee, he opened fire killing the first four guys with two or three shots in the center of each of their chests. He spun and knifed the next, as he swung his left hand with the pistol into the side of another's head knocking him to the ground. With several down, a shot rang out killing the next one as Logan charged into the free for all.

Hitting the group of men like a wild bull he screamed, "You bunch of low life assholes."

He picked up the next one by the throat and crotch and threw him into the rest. Looking around, he saw more coming and yelled to Joe, "Come on, let's get out of here."

Logan ran over a small hill as Joe spun to meet the newcomers. Firing two shots, he killed one and wounded another. Placing his thumb on the magazine release, he flicked his wrist and let the empty magazine fall to the ground as he slipped in a full magazine. Moving his thumb to the slide release, he was hit from behind. Dropping to his knees and falling forward into the desert sand, he slowly slid down a long tunnel into darkness.

Kay knew she was seriously out gunned. She had know idea where Logan and Rene were or if they were even still alive.

Hector and his gang executed a perfect raid and separated the four friends. Kay managed to grab a rifle as she ran for cover. Her .22/250 was flat shooting and deadly accurate.

As the gang of claim jumping, drug running, human trafficking slime charged into the camp, Joe yelled *run* but instead of running, he attacked giving the others a chance to escape.

She continued to move the scope from target to target. Suddenly she saw a flash of light coming from something or someone above and beyond where Joe was being held.

Hector drew back and punched Joe in the kidneys, dropping him to his knees just as a shot rang out. She watched as Juan grabbed his shoulder and then dropped from sight. Kay's finger tightened on the trigger as Hector ran for cover forgetting, momentarily, about Joe lying just a few feet away. She slowly squeezed the trigger.

Kay's shot was off just a couple of inches as the bullet hit him in the upper shoulder instead of where she was aiming-the center of his chest. He started turning and dropped just as the gun went off. That and that alone had saved his life. Kay was pissed beyond belief and had absolutely no patience left.

A smile came to her face as she saw Logan rise from behind a clump of brush and watched as he carefully and slowly crawled forward trying to get to where Joe was lying. She swung the scope back to where Hector had disappeared from sight just to see someone pop up. Slowly she squeezed off another shot hitting Pedro in the forearm just before he fired causing his shot to go wide. He screamed with pain as the .55 grain bullet hit his forearm at nearly 4000 feet per second. Tearing apart muscle and destroying bone.

Logan reached for Joe and grabbed him by the collar. Then throwing him over his shoulder into a fireman's carry. He ran back over the hill and dropped behind a dead tree for temporary safety as Kay and Rene both opened up picking target after target, keeping the would-be human trafficking, drug smuggling, claim jumping, human waste pinned down.

With deadly accurate shot placement, one by one the gang of human traffickers found themselves with holes God never intended for them to have and bleeding as the two women continued to pour cover fire trying to protect Logan and give him a chance to get to safety.

With Joe now free he and Logan started moving back toward the gold claim. Kay watched as Rene disappeared and reappeared, working her way towards where the guys had just disappeared only seconds before. Kay continued to find a few more targets of opportunity as she carefully scanned the area for anyone that was still moving. She watched as Rene tried to get closer to where Logan and Joe had disappeared.

Carefully Kay slid backwards from between the two rocks she had been using as cover and slowly started working her way around in the direction Logan and Joe had disappeared. As she maneuvered around a corner, she saw Logan standing with his hands up, watching as Santiago moved toward him with a pistol in his hand.

Kay slipped back and took a deep breath; she shouldered her rifle just as Rene walked in from the other side. She heard Santiago say, "Drop your gun and keep your hands where I can see them! Juan will pay dearly to get you. He's told us all that whoever captures you will be very well rewarded."

Kay slowly positioned herself; placing the crosshairs on the back of his head, she said, "Well, it won't be you. Don't even think about it. Or the next person you'll be talking to will be Satan. Just drop your gun before I blow your damn head off."

Santiago has no choice. Slowly he let his arm fall and his fingers released the pistol as it fell to the ground.

"Now kick it towards the others. I'm done running from Hector and Juan and the rest of you. If you so much as twitch, I'll put a bullet in your skull. You'll be out of this forever. I have something I want you to tell him and you are going to deliver the message."

Taking a deep breath, Kay looked around then back at Santiago.

Continuing she said, "He has pushed us for the last time and you are going to deliver a message to him and that dumb ass Juan. Now listen and listen good. If we so much as see any of you we'll start hunting, and we will shoot to kill. So far we have all been just trying to wound, hoping you would get the message and leave us alone. That ends and it ends now."

Kay continued to move forward toward Santiago. Sticking the barrel in his back, she pushed him forward. He slowly turned and gave Kay a look of peer loathing. That look pissed off Kay even more as she kicked Santiago's pistol towards Rene. Santiago looked around at his captives and sneered, "Hector wants you. He just takes what he wants and kills whoever is in the way."

Kay replied, "Well, I don't want him. He's nothing but a worthless piece of shit."

Kay took three quick steps forward and kicked Santiago in the nuts, dropping him doubled over to the ground. Looking down at him she said, "Do you think you can remember that or should I just put a bullet in your worthless ass and deliver your dead body to them or better yet just leave your just leave your sorry ass here, and let the buzzards have you?"

Santiago swallowed as he closed his eyes and said, "Yes, I'll remember."

"Good," replied Kay, "Now crawl back to that ass and tell him to either leave us alone or make his peace and to prepare to die."

Earlier that year

CHAPTER ONE

High in the Rocky Mountains Joe West laid in a sleeping bag. He's in an elk hunting drop camp. By the light of a nearby lantern, he thumbed through the pictures of Kay in his phone. After being alone for all those years, he met the one woman that not only tore down the wall he had built around himself, she had actually set up housekeeping and now lived in his heart.

Turning off the lantern, he pulled the sleeping bag up to cover his shoulders, rolled onto his side, and drifted off to sleep.

Randy Jackson worked his way along a ridge line in the mountains of northern Afghanistan. He's hunting the Taliban while they were hunting him. Growing up in the mountains of north central Pennsylvania, he became an excellent hunter and woodsman by the age of fourteen. By eighteen he found himself in the military being trained by the best of the best as a black ops hunter sniper. The military honed his natural abilities and helped him to become one of the deadliest hunter snipers to ever come out of Ft Bragg.

The last intel report he received said that Omar and his brother Iman were in the area. They were responsible for the brutal murder and beheading of several military personnel and civilians. The pentagon had put them at the top of the elimination list and that had become Randy's job.

Finding a rock overhang where he could look down at the village below, Randy set up his spotting scope as he carefully scanned the village. Looking at every male that came into sight and had finally spotted Omar. Taking out his rangefinder, he measured the distance. Five hundred fifty six yards. Randy looked through the scope, making the adjustment he needed and steadied the crosshairs on Omar's forehead. And slowly squeezed the trigger.

Joe's eyes snapped open. He was drenched in a cold sweat and gasping for air. Getting up, he walked out into the cool crisp Montana night and picked up a few pieces of wood. Stirring up the coals he tossed in a few pieces, and in a few minutes he had a crackling fire going. Sitting down, he stared into the flames as he relived several scenes from his past.

Rubbing his chest, he traced the scars and bullet wounds and thought about the mountains of Afghanistan and the jungles of Columbia and his fifteen years of nearly continuous black ops for the military and DEA. Now in the Federal Witness protection program, Could he really protect Kay from his past?

He had met Kay by total accident. It was instantaneous—they had fallen in love with each other, and the first kiss sealed the deal. They knew they had to be together.

Joe turned and headed down the last part of the trail; that'll bring him into the meadow leading home. His client had filled his tag on the second morning and decided to go home early. That gave Joe eight days to search for a Rocky Mountain bull elk with Kay before the next client would arrive.

Reaching for his cell, he pressed the number under Kay's name. Kay answered on the first ring, "I'm all packed and waiting for you."

Joe smiled as he thought about spending seven days in the mountains hunting with his wife and said, "I'll be there in about an hour. It'll take a few minutes to load the pack horse and get headed for camp. While I was up here scouting earlier this year, I set up another camp. I didn't tell anyone about it. Honey, we'll have to hurry to get there before dark."

Kay replied, "The pack horse and my horse are all loaded, saddled and ready. Logan and Rene stopped and helped me. I'm just walking out the door to head your way. I'll meet you in the meadow where the trail heads up that narrow pass into the Buffalo Valley."

Joe knew exactly where she was talking about; they had started naming parts of the Rocking L for different things that had happened. Buffalo Valley was the valley where Logan had risked his and CJ's life outrunning a stampeding herd of Buffalo to save Rene, from a very painful, very brutal death.

Joe continued to smile as he thought about the large herd of elk he had seen in the new area he had found earlier that year. He had kept it a secret knowing if the possibility came up, he was definitely going to take Kay up there. He had seen several nice bulls and at least two monstrous bulls Montana was known for.

As he came around the last turn in the trail, he saw Kay and that amazing black Arabian stallion she now rode.

He had gotten Midnight for her several months earlier, and he had turned out to be as well behaved as CJ. While CJ was still the dominant stallion mostly because he was a few years older. The two horses had spent several hours together. Both under saddle, while being ridden and in the pasture. A few minor skirmishes had taken place although nothing that had worried Logan.

Stopping, he watched as Kay rode closer and closer. The mane and tail of Midnight rippled in the breeze matching the movement of Kay's black hair flowing out from beneath her hat. He could see her beautiful smile grow as she approached. He smiled as he looked at her eyes. Joe had fallen in love with her the first time they met and knew if she would have him, he would marry her.

Dismounting he waited as Kay approached. He watched as his beautiful wife threw her leg over the saddle horn and slid from the saddle. Standing stone still Midnight nudged Kay forward with his nose as if to say, *I know I have to share you with him. So go kiss him and get it over with.*

Giggling Kay turns , looking at Midnight she says, "Yeah, yeah don't be so pushy," as she rubbed his nose.

Dropping the reins, she then walked into Joe's waiting arms and kissed him. They stood there kissing and hugging each other for a tad too long. Midnight pushed his nose between them, forcing them apart.

Joe reached out and patted his neck as Midnight lifted his head and arched neck. Then lifting his tail into that amazing stance that Arabian horses are known for.

Kay patted his neck and ordered, "That's enough. Yes, we know you are jealous, but you will just have to learn to deal with it. He's my husband, and I love him."

Midnight whinnied and tossed his head. Joe started to laugh and said, "I think he understands you and doesn't like that idea."

Kay replied, "He may have, although he has no choice. He'll have to learn to deal with it."

Walking back to Joe, she pushed up onto her toes and kissed him again long and deep. Joe kept one eye on Midnight who had turned and looked the other way.

Joe laughed, "You know I really think he's jealous. When you went up on your toes to kiss me. He looked the other way."

Walking back to her horse, Kay patted his neck, put her foot into the stirrup, and said, "Let's get going. I really want to get there before dark and spend some quiet time with you."

Patting Midnight's neck again she continued, "Out of this pain in the neck's sight and reach."

Joe swung into the saddle and together they headed for the mountain trail that would bring them to Buffalo Valley and beyond into the high country where Joe feels most at home. He looked forward to getting to camp where he'd get to spend seven wonderful days alone with his wife.

Just as the day slowly started turning to night, they arrived in camp. Joe quickly built a fire and started removing the saddles from the horses. He turned them loose in the corral and threw in a full bail of hay. Next he started unloading the pack horse and put him in with the other two. Kay was cooking supper over the campfire, and after they ate, they made sure everything was cleaned up and put away. She made a couple cups of tea, and they settled in for a quiet evening... just the two of them.

Kay reached over and put her hand on Joe's leg and said, "I'm about done. I think we had better get some sleep if you plan on hunting tomorrow."

Smiling, he reached over and gave her a light kiss. Joe grabbed a high power light and walked over to check the horses. He made sure the poles in the gate were secure.

He walked into the tent and saw that Kay had placed both pistols on white towels next to the air mattress. She had also propped both rifles against the inside wood pile. Joe reached behind the camp box in the tent and picked up a short barrel 12 gauge shotgun working the action, he loaded a three inch magnum slug into the chamber. He knew there were four more slugs behind it, then two single ott buckshot. Putting the shotgun within easy reach, he smiled as he slid in next to Kay and felt her naked body press up against him.

They hadn't spent more than a couple of nights together in over a month. Joe was in charge of the entire outfitters business plus guiding hunters everyday. It was a very busy time of year.

Kay rolled into Joe's arms as their lips met and tongues started that romantic slow waltz that brought forward all the passion two people in love can share. His hands slid up and down her back as the passion grew. Soon Kay's hand started its ever so slow slide down his chest and stomach. Stopping just below his navel, she started sliding back up until she touched his jaw.

Joe's hand cupped her very shapely backside and continued down and around finding the inside of her thigh. He slowly slid his hand up and down several times, each time moving just a little higher than the time before.

Kay continued to slide her hand up then down his chest as her tongue danced with Joe's finding what she was looking for. She slowly started to slide her hand up and down.

Joe let out a low soft moan as she continued stroking him. With two fingers working inside, his thumb massaged her clitoris. It was Kay's turn to moan. She felt the wave slowly start to build, roll, and build again rolling faster and faster. Her breathing started to come in short gasps as her tongue slowed from the waltz to a slow dance simply moving in a circle. The wave continued to build and just when she thought it couldn't build any higher, it rolled and exploded into a body shuddering crash. As soon as the crash slowed, another wave started. It built and rolled and built and rolled again and again. Just as it reached its peak, the release came.

"Oh, my god. Oh, god," she cried out.

Joe smiled slightly as he continued working her into a frenzy. He kissed her just below her ear leaving a row of light tender kisses, nibbles, and bites continuing down her neck across her throat and up the other side. He mixed in a few moments of tender sucking at the base of her neck and reached around the back of her neck as far as possible without stopping what his hands were doing.

Kay slipped her arms around and slowly started to pull him on top of her. She felt the security as his weight settled. She wrapped her legs around him, loving the feeling that only he had ever given her—the complete feeling of loving a man with every ounce of her being with the knowledge that he loved her the same way completely and all the way through. It was something she had never felt in her life, something only Joe had ever brought to her and made her feel.

Joe loved the feeling that Kay gave him. She had been the only woman to penetrate the wall he had built. Although more than that, she managed to stay inside that wall and get into his heart—a place no other woman had ever gotten before. His body sensed the feeling as Kay's arms held him. It was the feeling of warmth, security, and love. It was the kind of love that passed between two people with a deep connection in their heart, mind, and soul.

Joe loved the feeling of Kay's legs slowly sliding up his sides, the feeling of love as a woman willingly gives herself to the man she loves and opens her mind and body to accept the pleasure he can give her.

Joe pushed into her and the movement started. Within seconds, she was in perfect time meeting each thrust. The wave started deep inside slowly and rolled towards the surface. Her breath came in short gasps and grew rolling over and building higher and higher. As the crash came, she felt Joe release and the movement slowed. They both laid gasping for air and holding each other.

Joe tried to roll away, but Kay hugged him even tighter, holding him in place and said, "No, stay here a little longer."

With her arms and legs still wrapped around him, Joe continued to kiss and nibble on her neck.

Soon a change started as Joe continued to kiss, nibble, and suck on Kay's neck shoulders and nipples. Kay arched her back to accept him. Her eyes rolled back as the first wave started. Kay rode the wave enjoying the slow steady build until the crash came in a body shuddering explosion of pleasure. With her body trembling, waiting, and anticipating, the next wave started. She felt it start deep inside as Joe's motions increased. The wave moved toward the surface at an incredible rate. It built and rolled and built higher and higher.

Kay cried, "Oh, oh, oh, oh, god," as she released and felt Joe release just seconds later.

With her arms and legs still wrapped around him, she held him trying to breathe and not wanting him to move. Joe slowly pushed himself up as Kay let him go and rolled to the side as he wrapped his arms around her. They laid quietly just feeling the love they shared and knowing they were God's gift to each other. Their meeting and marriage was meant to be.

Lying in Joe's arms was Kay's absolute favorite place. She would fold into him and simply enjoy the closeness. She felt it as he sensed her movement, making a slight change in his position to make sure she was totally and completely comfortable. It was all the little things he did that had caused her to fall so deeply and madly in love with him— helping her with her coat, opening doors, walking on the outside and a half step behind her to protect her from danger, and always, absolutely always, putting her needs ahead of his own.

Just like always, Joe's eyes flickered open just before five in the morning.

He laid there a few minutes enjoying the closeness of his wife lying next to him. Then carefully he slid out of bed. Joe seldom if ever would roll over and go back to sleep although there were occasions when Kay had convinced him to come back to bed. On those occasions, Kay was always right.

Getting dressed he turned and looked back at Kay still asleep. He smiled and thought, *how could I get so lucky as to have a woman as beautiful and loving yet down to earth and practical as her to fall in love with me?*

Walking to the tent opening he looked east into the mountains and the sunrise and thought about what her boss had said when Kay retired from the magazine, "The mountain man and the lady."

Glancing at the surrounding mountains he thought, *yeah I most certainly love it up here.* Then looking back at Kay he smiled and thought, *if it wasn't for her I'd come up here and stay although now my place is where she is.*

Pushing the coals around in the fire ring, he placed a few small pieces of wood and watched as they started to burn. He tossed a few larger ones on the pile and slid the cooking grate over the fire to get the coffee started.

He checked the horse's water and tossed in a bail of hay. Looking across the valley, he could now see the target he set up to check rifles. Walking back to the fire, he poured two cups and headed into the tent.

Sitting down next to Kay, he sipped his coffee while holding the other cup close to her. He watched as her nose slowly started to wake as the aroma of the coffee invaded her senses and interrupted her dreams. As her eyes started to flicker she woke and said, "Good morning."

That beautiful smile crossed her lips…the smile that Joe loved to see. It's all in the way she said good morning that makes it so special to him.

Kay was waking up slowly, as Joe started preparing breakfast. It was time for a shower for Kay, and that consisted of water heated over the fire and poured into a water bag that hung from a tree branch. Joe placed a pallet on the ground and hung a tarp from a couple of poles to give her some privacy.

Soon she joined him. He poured her another cup and handed her bacon and eggs with pan fried potatoes and toast made over the fire. Kay smiled as she looked at Joe's toaster. It looked like a tennis racket, only it's all wire and had two sides. He put a couple pieces of bread in it, closed the top and held it over the flames for a few seconds. He rolled it over and a few seconds later he had perfect camp toast every time.

With breakfast done and everything cleaned up, Joe grabbed both rifles and walked over to the sight-in area. He loaded Kay's rifle and looked through the scope. He touched the button and the red dot instantly appeared. Taking a deep breath and letting it half out, he slowly squeezed the trigger. Looking at the target through the scope he thought," I sure like these shoot-&-see targets." He could see where the bullet hit without the aid of a spotting scope. Two inches high and an inch to the right at two hundred yards. Making a slight adjustment, he loaded another round and slowly squeezed the trigger.

"Close enough," he said as he looked at the new hole two inches high of dead center.

Handing the gun to Kay he smiled and said, "Here you go. Two inches high and dead center at two hundred yards."

Picking up his rifle and slipping a shell into the chamber, he touched the button and slowly squeezed the trigger. Still looking through his scope at his target. His shot was nearly touching the second shot from Kay's rifle.

Looking at Kay, he said, "So, should we go hunting?"

Walking back to where the horses were saddled and waiting, Joe slipped his rifle into the rifle scabbard hanging from the saddle. Taking up both sets of reins he led the horses back to where Kay was just stepping out of the tent. Joe dropped the reins as he slipped Kay's rifle into the scabbard on her saddle. Checking his saddle bags, he took a quick inventory. Looking into Kay's saddle bags he saw that she had already packed their lunch.

Glancing back at Kay, he asked, "Are we ready?"

Kay replied with a huge smile, " Ready? Are you kidding? I've been waiting for this for a couple of months. My god yes. Let's go."

The pair mounted the horses and headed up and over the top of the horizon, dipping into another valley. They came out on a point and dismounted, raising their binoculars up to their eyes and surveying the valley and surrounding mountain side.

"Hey, Joe. There's a small herd over there," said Kay, peering into her binoculars and pointing to a blur in the distance, "There's one bull that looks pretty nice."

Joe quickly set up a spotting scope and said, "Yes, he is a very nice bull. Let's save him for next Thursday. Let's just leave them alone. They won't go far and we can always find them again. I've seen a couple of monster bulls around here. That's what I want to try to find first."

They spent the rest of the day riding and glassing valley after valley, stopping at all of the small natural meadows Joe found. Hundreds of elk and several nice shooter bulls crossed their paths, however they didn't see any of the bulls Joe was looking for. He so badly wanted to find one of the huge bulls. The type of bull Montana was known for. He wanted that chance for Kay. The opportunity to get a true trophy Rocky Mountain bull elk. He was absolutely positive they were still in the area, at least, as far as he knew. It was about a two or three hour ride from the closest camp they had previously set up- no one else had been back this far or knew about the camp.

Joe and Kay rode back into camp just before dark. In the matter of a half hour a fire was crackling and Kay had started supper. Joe unsaddled the horses and turned them into the corral, tossing them a bale of hay and filling their water. He grabbed a brush and gave all three horses a good rub down, brushing away the remains of their tiresome day. Joe and Kay walked back to the fire together and sat down, enjoying a fantastic meal cooked over a fire and another quiet evening under the stars.

Kay slid a pot of water over the fire to boil and made them each a cup of tea.

Settling in next to Joe, she asked, "Hon, is something bothering you? What are you thinking about?"

"I've been thinking about this area and where those two huge bulls would go," Joe replied, "I'm absolutely sure they wouldn't leave. They have everything they want. I mean just look, they have all the food and water they could ask for. Plus there's absolutely no hunting pressure," Joe paused and stared into the fire before adding, "there's another valley up over that mountain," he pointed back behind where they were camped, "maybe tomorrow we should try to work our way back there. The trail is narrow, not much more than a game trail." He glanced in the direction of the corral. "Do you think Midnight will behave? It's really narrow and there are a few places where we might have to lead the horses."

Kay looked into the black Montana night and said, "I've ridden him all over the ranch, although I haven't come back this far. I've been on a few narrow trails and he's always been really calm. I'm sure he'll be okay."

Joe smiled and kissed her. "Okay, let's get some sleep. Tomorrow is going to be a very long day."

As alway Joe's eyes opened just before 5am. He laid there for a few extra minutes, enjoying the feeling of Kay being so close. He slowly slipped out of bed. After getting dressed he got the fire going and started coffee. He walked across to the corral and checked the horses, feeding them and giving them more water.

He poured the first cup and thought about the trail to the valley, south west of where they were camped. He's walked that trail a couple of times. Glancing over at the horses he said, "You three had better be good."

Walking back to the corral he scratched Midnight behind the ears and reasoned, "We need to come to an understanding. I know you love her and would do most everything she asks. Well, I love her, too, and remember, I bought you for her. So, you had better be good today. If she gets hurt because of you, well, let's put it this way, you won't be a happy horse. So, no shenanigans and I mean it. Absolutely no screwing around on that trail today. Understand?"

Noticing his coffee was gone, he walked back to the fire just as Kay walked out of the tent fully dressed and ready to go. In a few minutes bacon was sizzling in the frypan. Kay sat down and was enjoying her morning coffee. Before light they were in the saddle and headed out for a day of hunting, but more than that, it was mostly a day of just being together.

As they neared the point where the trail broke over a ridge and headed down into the valley, Joe stopped. Dismounting, he grabbed his binoculars and walked to the ridge line. Looking at the valley below and the mountains on both sides, He heard footsteps and turned as Kay walked up behind him and said, "Anything down there?"

Joe replied," Yes." As he walked towards a grassy knoll. Sitting down in the grass Joe laid his rifle across his lap as he continued glassing the the valley below.

Joe pointed and said softly," Hey look over that way. There's a good size herd in that clearing. Plus, I just watched a really nice bull walk across this meadow and into the timber. I didn't get a real good look at him, but I think he might be one of the two big bulls I saw earlier this year. I have seen movement in the timber. I think he may have moved his herd there although there's always the chance that there's more than the two I saw. This area is big enough to hold several of those monster bulls."

Kay asked, "How can we set up on him?"

Joe looked around and said, "Let's leave the horses here and walk that ridge line and see if there's a place where you can see most of this area and across to that other ridge."

Kay quickly stretched a rope for a picket line as Joe unsaddled and tied all three horses. Grabbing their rifles, they headed across the mountain side and started down the ridge. Finding a small point, Joe picked up a few rocks and pulled down a half down tree. Then taking a few rocks and short chunks of logs, he made a spot where Kay could get a firm shooting rest. Taking his rifle, he began using the laser range finder to check distances.

Turning to Kay he said, "It's just over 500 yards all the way across. If that bull goes that way, it'll be a long shot, but you have hit at that distance at home. So, take your time and put a hole in him. If you knock him down. I'll find him."

Looking around for a minute he pointed and said, "I'm going to go back to where we left the horses and walk out on that ridge. If I can't see him in there I'll drop off and try and push him out. He should either go around me and up that far side or come out towards you. If he goes up that far side, hit him as many times as you can. I'm going to drop way down so he can't go down hill. He'll have to go up that far side or come right to you. Now one more thing. Try and count his points. The two I saw. One is a six by seven and the other is a seven by seven. So try and count if he doesn't have at least seven on one side don't shoot. He's not one of the bulls that we are looking for."

Joe reached over and gave her a quick kiss. He headed back up the ridge and around to the other side while watching the ravine for movement. As he neared the point where the ridge fell away he saw movement. He carefully scanned the area and saw a giant set of antlers move through the timber, dropping off the ridge, and head into the ravine.

Moving as quickly as possible while still trying to be quiet Joe watched as the antlers turned and headed up the far side of the valley. Shouldering his rifle he touched the button. The red dot instantly appeared and after looking at the information at the top, Joe put the dot between the bulls shoulders. Just as he began to take a deep breath he heard Kay's .270 echo through the ravine. Joe watched as the huge bull stumbled and headed down the hill. Kay's rifle sounded for a second time just as the bull in Joe's crosshairs fell from sight.

He thought he heard Kay scream, "Yes! Yes! Joe, he's down! He's down!"

Joe started the steep uphill climb and worked his way around to where he could see Kay. She was pointing down and ahead of him. She had done exactly what he had told her. *Stay where you shot from. Pick something close to where the animal was standing when you shot and wait. I'll come to you, just wait.* Joe kept working along the side of the mountain trying to get to where Kay was pointing.

"He was by the rock!" Joe heard her exclaim.

Joe looked at all the huge boulders. "What one?" he yelled out.

Kay responded, "The one with the tree stump. He was just above the stump and looking back into the ravine when I hit him the first time."

Joe closed his eyes for a minute and tried to recall the sight in the scope when Kay had fired. The bull had been standing close to a ragged stump. Joe continued forward walking from boulder to boulder looking for a ragged stump when he spotted the blood trail. Leaving his hat there he followed the trail and saw the stump. Turning, Joe motioned for Kay to climb down and join him.

Joe sat on a rock and waited as Kay made her way down the mountain side. As she approached he said, "I've got his trail here. He won't go far plus I saw you hit him the second time. I'm sure he's just inside the timber." Looking back up the mountain side he said, "It's going to take several hours getting that brute to where we left the horses. In my saddle bags are several meat sacks. I'll cut him up and use a backpack to get him to the horses. Then we can hang the meat in trees tonight and finish getting it out tomorrow."

"Nope," she replied, "We can go get the horses and bring them most of the way here. Just around that point is the trail and a level spot about twenty-by-twenty. While I was waiting and watching you work around to that side. I walked over and looked into the valley and saw the trail."

Joe looked back at her and asked, "Why were you walking around?"

"Umm…I- I- had to pee. So I walked over there. I was by that tree," as she pointed towards a nearby tree, "when I saw his antlers. My pants were still down and my gun was leaning against that tree up there."

Joe looked to his right and uphill as he replied, "I think from now on you had better wear Depends or something like that. I'm sure I would have died laughing if I'd seen you trying to get your pants up and to your rifle at the same time. All the while trying to be quiet and not spook that bull." He stood up and walked over to kiss her. "Oh god I love you. You just saved me climbing out of here about eight or more times and to think. It's just because you had too much coffee this morning. Hey by chance did you count his points?"

Kay laughed and replied, "Absolutely, I counted seven on one side. Twice just before I pulled the trigger."

Joe looked at the trail and then at Kay. Reaching over he kissed her again and said, "Let's go find your bull."

Together they started following the trail. Joe stayed on the downhill side of the trail with Kay slightly below him and a couple of yards behind. With him being left-handed and her right-handed their aiming swings wouldn't cross, bringing the other into the sight picture.

Soon they could see where the bull had entered the timber. Joe said, "Wait here just in case he's not down and breaks out this way."

Joe worked his way into the timber and in a few minutes he called to Kay to join him. Joe could see the bull laying at the base of a huge old cedar just fifty or sixty feet away.

As Kay walked up, Joe pointed and said, "He's right over there. I'm sure he's done. I've been watching him for a good five minutes. You lead. Poke him with your rifle barrel a few times before walking in front of him and that set of daggers attached to his head."

Joe slung his rifle over his shoulder and pulled out his phone. He touched the camera app and started taking pictures as Kay walked up to a monstrous Montana bull elk. He continued to take pictures as she pulled the head around and started touching each of the fourteen points. Looking at Joe she asked, "Is this a nice elk?"

Joe nodded his head and said, "Oh my god, yes. It's a very nice one."

"Is it bigger than the one you have hanging over the fireplace?" Kay asked.

"Oh, absolutely honey. I'm quite sure it is," Joe answered.

"Can we get it mounted?"

Joe replied, "Of course we can. I'll cape it out right here. I'll take my time and make sure it's right."

Kay asked, "Where can we put it?"

Joe replied, "Anyplace you want. Do you have a place already picked out?"

Joe grabbed a back leg and started to pull the huge animal around to get the head higher than the rear end when Kay said, "I would like to put it over the fireplace where yours is."

He took his knife out and started to field dress and said, "Yes, that would be ok. Where should we put mine? Hey come here and hold this leg out of my way. But keep your rifle in your hands. This is bear country and those two shots are like ringing a dinner bell."

Kay grabbed the leg and pulled. She said, "I don't know, maybe out in your shop. We don't need that little one in the house anymore."

Joe looked up and saw Kay laughing so hard that she started shaking. Joe started to laugh too and said, "Oh really?"

Kay replies, "Well it wouldn't look very big with this one hanging close by."

Still laughing, Joe said, "We can put mine somewhere. Where you can't see them both."

With that devilish grin Kay said, "That's why I suggested your shop."

Joe stood up, stretched, and took the three steps to where Kay was standing. Kissing his wife and asking, "Should we move that six-by-six mule deer out there also?"

"Oh, no sweetheart, it can stay where it is." Smiling, Kay continued, "Until I get a bigger one."

As she breaks out laughing again.

Joe shook his head and kissed her and looked back at the job at hand. Pushing the rear leg back to Kay he said, "Now hold this. We really need to get this done."

Kay grabbed the leg as Joe went back to work. Glancing up he saw that she had her rifle laying across her arm. Then after looking around he saw his standing against a tree just a few feet away. Looking back at what he's doing he started again.

Kay was looking behind her and then back again at Joe. As he got to the final part, Kay heard a branch snap. Looking up she saw another huge bull walking towards them. Carefully she hooked her leg around the elk's leg and shouldered her rifle.

It all happened in a few seconds. Kay pulled the trigger. The recoil knocked her off-balance where she had no choice but to move her leg to keep from falling over. The weight loaded rear leg of the bull she was holding snapped closed, hitting Joe and knocking him off balance and into the gut pile.

Joe started pushing himself up as he yelled, "What the hell are you shooting at?"

Just as Kay squeezed the trigger for the second time, Joe's hand slipped in the mud and he fell face-first back into the yuck again. Scrabbling, he finally pushed himself away from the mess.

Looking back at Kay who was trying hard not to laugh at Joe sitting on his rump with a really stupid look on his face and a huge mud and blood stain on the side of his jaw, neck and shoulder where the weight loaded leg had hit him, knocking him sideways.

Again, Joe asked, "What are you shooting at?"

Kay shrunk down. "Another bull elk came through. I watched him fall just over there. Ummm…I just…umm…I-I- umm I just killed another really big bull."

Joe started to laugh as he said, "You're kidding right?"

Kay gave a small smile and replied, "Nope," pointing she continued, "he's just over there."

With a smile Joe said, "You know we are staying here tonight."

"I put two sleeping bags and some minimal supplies on the pack horse. We should have enough to survive. Although I didn't bring much in the way of meat." She smiled and added, "Although I took care of that. We should have more than enough now."

Joe stood up and shook his head. "Yes you certainly did. Now here, hold this." Then looking up he started to laugh and said, "Don't let go and for Christ's sake don't shoot another one. We don't have any tags left."

With the first elk done for now Joe grabbed his rifle and backpack and said, "I'm not sure if I should call you Annie Oakley or Calamity Jane. Either way let's go find your other bull."

They started walking together with Joe in the lead. He heard Kay say, "To your right, hon. He was standing by that dead tree."

Joe pointed. "That tree?"

"Yes, that's where I hit him the first time," she replied.

Joe walked to the tree. "Come on, here's the trail." He waited for Kay, watching her walk towards him with the brightest smile he had ever seen. "Wow," he thought, "she is one happy lady."

They walked about two hundred yards before Kay pointed out the bull. Joe looked over, then slung his rifle over his shoulder as he grabbed his phone. He took several more pictures of Kay touching each of the twelve points. The second elk wasn't the seven-by-six Joe had seen earlier that year. Although the bull was still a huge six-by-six, with extremely heavy bases, long heavy main beams, and long points. Joe smiled as he watched his wife run her fingers and hands along the main beams and points. He continued to take pictures. Finally reaching for his knife he said, "Here, honey, hold this. Don't you dare let go of his leg. Or you'll be doing this. Oh, and keep your eyes open. Mostly that way," as he pointed down wind.

Two hours later Joe had both elk cut into quarters. It was late in the afternoon by the time they climbed to where the horses were. The horses were. So tired that they looked dead. Joe grabbed another canteen of water. He sat down as Kay walked over to him and whispered in his ear, "I know you're tired, but if you can get that mud and blood off your neck, I'll be really nice to you tonight."

Joe started to laugh and said, "You're going to be really nice to me regardless." He kissed her and took another long drink. Then he stood up and started to saddle and load the horses.

By working together Joe and Kay managed to get both of the elk into camp just before dark. Kay started to cook supper while Joe deboned the meat and put it into game bags. While they worked they talked about the day hunt and the fact that Kay had shot two of the largest elk Joe had seen in a long time. Taking it a couple hundred yards away from camp Joe finally got the last of the elk up and hanging from the branches high in a tree. He did his best to clean up with the water they had, while also trying to save enough for coffee the next morning. Finally, totally exhausted he walked back to the fire and sat down next to Kay.

Joe could see both rifles standing against the rock wall next to where Kay had laid out their sleeping bags. Her pistol was lying next to where she would be sleeping while Joe's was still around his waist.

Kay started to prepare plates and sat down to enjoy supper. They ate fresh elk backstrap cooked over campfire pan fried potatoes. After supper they sat talking about the hunt. Joe said, "I don't think I ever saw that second elk. He was a huge six-by-six. I'm sure he'll measure 350 inches plus." He glanced up at the two racks illuminated by the light of the campfire. "I'm going to keep this area back here a secret. In fact, when we break camp, I'll leave most of not all the equipment here. I brought it all up in weatherproof containers."

"So this will become our getaway area?" Kay asked.

Joe asked, "Would you like that? Our own little spot where we can come and just hide from the world and all the stupid shit going on?"

Kay reached over and kissed his cheek. She replied, "Any place you are is our hideaway." She smiled and asked, "Are there any mule deer back here?"

Joe started to laugh and said, "Yes, honey, I'm quite sure there are."

"Any really big mule deer?" she asked.

"Yes, honey," he answered. "I was through this area following the women last summer and when I wasn't watching them I would glass the mountains. There are also bighorn sheep and mountain goats." He paused and looked at her as the light from the fire danced in her eyes. "Why? What are you thinking?"

Kay snuggled a little close and said, "Oh, there's just a spot in the house where I would really like to put a bigger one." She exploded into laughter.

Joe laughed and pulled her closer. He hugged her and said, "Okay Calamity Kay, let's get some sleep. My tank is absolutely empty."

He slowly got up and walked over to check on the horses one more time, making sure all three were securely tied to the picket line. He then divided the remaining hay he had brought down on the pack horse between the three of them. Once the horses were fed he walked back and undressed slowly, slipping into the sleeping bag and feeling the warmth of Kay's body. He smiled as he laid there, chuckling softly about the day's events.

Morning was cool and clear. Joe thought he smelt something. The fog slowly cleared as the aroma of fresh coffee invaded his system. Someone had put the coffee on. He moved his arm and found an empty spot where Kay should have been. His eyes slowly opened and his system came alive. Coffee and bacon. Joe opened his eyes to a beautiful Montana high country morning with Kay sitting next to him with a cup of coffee and that beautiful morning smile.

He sat up and reached for the coffee as Kay leaned forward and kissed him. Then she put her hand against the side of his neck. Joe flinched as the pain shot through him and said, "Ouch! Damn girl, what did you touch?"

"You have a huge black and blue spot on the lower part of your jaw and neck," Kay replied.

Joe moved his hand and softly touched his jaw. He could feel where his jaw was swollen and the area beneath it was very tender. "Yeah," he replied, "that's where I got clubbed yesterday when you let go of the elk's leg."

"Oh, hon," Kay said apologetically, "I'm so sorry! I didn't think that would happen or I would have never shot at the second bull."

Joe smiled and said, "It was worth it. Just to see the smile on your face I would take another ass whopping." He got up and continued, "I'm going to call Logan and have him meet us in Buffalo Valley. That'll make getting both of these home a lot easier." He opened his saddle bags and powered up his satellite phone, pressing Logan's number.

Logan answered saying, "Hey, buddy. How's the hunting going?"

"Absolutely fantastic," Joe replied. "Hey, can you meet us in Buffalo Valley in three hours? We have two really big bulls and only one pack horse. There's absolutely no way he can haul both out."

"Absolutely. Should I bring one or two horses?"

Joe thought for a minute and said, "It's a steep climb out of here. Bring two that'll make it easier and less of a load for the horses."

"Alright, see you at noon," Logan said.

Four hours later Joe and Kay were sitting in the shade of the big old tree they camped by several months earlier while chasing a group of human traffickers. Logan rode up followed by Rene and two empty pack horses. "Wow. Hey, Joe. What the hell happened to you?" Logan said.

Joe reached up to carefully rub his neck and jaw and then looked at Kay. "Ask Calamity Kay over there."

"Ask who?" Logan and Rene asked at the same time.

"Umm that would be me," Kay said.

Joe started to laugh and said, "I saw the first bull. It took about an hour to get set up on him. I watched Anne Oakley over here," he pointed at Kay and continued, "put two nice shots in him and he tipped over just two hundred yards from where she hit him the second time. After that it gets really stupid."

"Okay, I'm waiting," Logan replied.

"Yeah, me too," said Rene.

"Well Joe asked me to hold a rear leg while he field dressed the first one. So I'm standing there looking around when I hear a branch break. At first I thought it might be a bear. So I hooked my leg around the elk's leg and kept watching." As she's told the story she got more and more animated with her arms flying and facial expressions. Pausing to catch her breath she continued, "When a huge six-point walked to within fifty yards of where we are. I aimed and fired, hitting him. The recoil knocked me off balance and I had to move my leg to keep from falling over backwards. As I took the second shot I heard Joe swear and then ask what the hell I was shooting at. Looking back I saw him trying to push himself out of the gut pile he had just removed from the first elk. Then I told him I had shot another, while trying so hard not to laugh. You should have seen the look on his face- it was absolutely priceless. First he's slipping and sliding trying to get up and see what's happening. Then I say I shot another and it went from confusion to total bewilderment."

By now Logan was laughing so hard he could barely stay in the saddle. Rene was not that lucky and she slid sideways, catching the saddle horn. Then her knees buckled and she hunched over into the grass, holding onto her stomach.

Joe was about to tip forward. He was nearly out of the saddle. He was holding his stomach and could barely breathe. "So I'm not sure if we should call her Calamity Kay or Kay Oakley."

The four friends stood there talking and laughing about what had happened in a place now named by Joe as Calamity Kay Valley.

Kay asked, "Would you two like to eat with us before heading back?"

"Absolutely," Rene replied, as she walked with Kay towards the horses and some of their supplies.

Logan walked around and gathered firewood as Joe started a fire. In a few minutes Kay and Rene had lunch cooking. Logan reached into his saddle bags and pulled out four bottles of beer.

"That's what I heard tinkling on the way up here," said Rene. "I was looking around trying to figure out what it was." Laughter once again exploded around the campfire.

Two hours later with everything cleaned up Logan and Rene swung into the saddles and headed for home with the first of Kay's two huge Montana bull elk. While Joe and Kay headed back up into the high country to get the other one, along with the two capes and antlers.

They got both pack horses loaded in an hour and headed towards home when Joe said, "I think we'll be staying in Buffalo Valley tonight. There's no way we can get over that mountain trail before dark and I really don't want to try it after dark."

They arrived in the valley and stopped under the same tree to set up camp. Joe unloaded and unsaddled the horses. He got them tied to the picket line and quickly got the fire started. Kay began super as Joe continued to collect firewood.

With supper nearly done and enough wood to last the night, Joe set up the tent and Kay put the sleeping bags inside. Joe grabbed both rifles and placed them inside of the tent.

Kay started dishing up supper and looked around to see Joe walking back from the creek with two bottles of beer. It was the same creek and pool they had gone skinny dipping in last summer. She smiled and asked, "Now where did you find those?"

"Logan had four left," Joe replied. "He gave them to me and I put them in the creek before we left. I already knew we would be staying here tonight." He opened the first and handed it to Kay as he sat down next to her.

With supper done and everything cleaned up, Joe got up and used the light on his phone. He was back in a few minutes with two more beers. Together they sat by the fire and enjoyed their beers as they talked and laughed about their first real hunting trip together. Tenderly touching his jaw, Joe said, "I'm quite sure I'll remember this hunt for years to come." He laughed. "Many years to come."

Kay snuggled up under his shoulder and said, "I'm really sorry."

"It's okay, honey. I'd do it all over again just to see your smile."

Kay kissed his cheek. As one they stood up. Kay went into the tent while Joe banked the fire and added a few more of the bigger pieces. Then he walked over to check on the horses. Returning to the campfire he put the four empty bottles where he could find them in the morning.

He got undressed, went into the tent, and slipped in next to Kay. Taking her in his arms he pulled her close and whispered, "I love you."

Kay rolled in his arms, kissed him, and replied, "I love you too." She snuggled a little closer and they were soon fast asleep.

Joe's eyes snapped open. Something was moving around just outside the tent. Ever so slowly his hand found the .44 magnum laying next to him. He slowly set it up and slipped out of the sleeping bag. Still not sure if it was dangerous or not, he tried not to startle Kay. He moved so he could open the tent flap with his right hand and had the pistol ready in his left hand as he peered out to see a grizzly sniffing around. Joe's hand found Kay's leg and he slowly shook her awake. With a full moon and a cloudless sky there was enough light so Kay could see him motion to be still. Slowly he got into a crouching position and jumped outside the tent screaming at the top of his lungs and jumping around like a deranged lunatic while holding the pistol in both hands leveled at the bear.

The startled bear grunted, growled, and farted, taking off running across the valley and away from the smell of meat and whatever was making all the racket. Joe quickly got dressed and in a few minutes he was out checking to make sure the horses didn't run off and that the bear didn't destroy anything.

He threw several more pieces of wood onto the fire and slid the cooking grate into place. Then he walked to the pool and filled the coffee pot with fresh water. Putting the pot over the fire to boil he saw Kay come out of the tent.

Looking at Joe she asked, "Was it a bear?"

"Yeah, but a young one I think. Be careful walking around. I think I scared the shit out of him. I heard him grunt, growl, and fart as he lit out across the valley. I walked over there a few steps and it stinks."

Kay started to laugh and said, "Only you could scare the crap out of a bear. What do you want for breakfast and hey, pour me a cup of that coffee," as she starts looking through their leftover supplies.

Joe poured a second cup and walked over to where Kay was trying to find something for breakfast as he reached down and grabbed her by the belt. He lifted her into a standing position as he handed her the coffee. Then he pulled her closer and smiled, kissing her and saying, "Anything you want to make works for me, Calamity Kay."

Kay started to laugh and said, "I like Kay Oakley better."

Joe smiled as he replied, "Yeah, I know. Just remember that I love you." He reached out and pulled her closer, giving her one of those kisses designed to make you weak in the knees and looking for a bed. Kay responded like she always did when the man she loved was kissing her that way. She simply melted into the moment as did Joe. Nothing else mattered except what was happening between them at that moment.

As they came up for air, Joe said, "I think we need a bed."

Kay took a deep settling breath and replied, "Yes, we do, and there's one about twenty-five miles that way." She pointed towards home.

They walked back to the fire. Kay grabbed the frying pan and tossed the remaining bacon in with several pieces of elk meat. Then placed it on the cooking grate. Next, she chopped up the last half of an onion, green pepper, and two potatoes they had. Looking one more time she found a small container of mushrooms. She handed it to Joe to open and placed it along with everything else back in the pan. Then he added the mushrooms and started to slowly mix everything together. After about fifteen minutes she added the last four eggs. She scrambled the eggs, mixing everything together one more time.

Ten minutes later they were enjoying a Rocky Mountain scramble cooked Western style over an open campfire. Joe took a mouth full as he pointed out a large herd of elk feeding their way through the valley. They watched as the herd bull kept chasing the smaller bulls away from his ladies as they sat there eating breakfast.

Joe said, "The rut is over. Although he'll keep that herd together for a couple more weeks before he simply loses interest and wanders off to spend the winter either alone or with a bachelor herd somewhere. Come next fall this will start all over again. He'll only be a herd bull for a few years before another bull of his size or bigger and stronger will come along. They'll meet and fight. The winner of that battle will take control of the herd of females. Only the strongest get to pass on their genetics."

"Are the fights brutal?" Kay asked.

"Oh, absolutely," Joe replied. "They are really big animals and those antlers are sharp and strong. I've seen them break off another bull's antlers, break legs, or even puncture each other."

Dumping the last of his coffee Joe said, "Come on, Calamity. Let's go home. I've still got to cut and wrap all of this meat. Get your two elk to the taxidermy shop. Plus I have a few more clients to take hunting this year."

They arrived home several hours later. Joe and Kay had the horses unsaddled and unloaded and in the barn. After feeding them, Kay gave them all a good brushing. Joe got all of the meat hanging in the walk-in cooler in his shop. All of the camping supplies they had brought off the mountain were cleaned and put away. The last thing outside was to get the saddles and pack saddles, put away bridles, and close the barn for the night.

"Tomorrow's another day," he thought as he walked towards the house. Meeting Kay at the door he said, "Give me five minutes to relax and I'll help you with whatever is left."

Kay handed him one of the two beers she was holding and replied, "I'm done. Clothes are in the washer. Rifles and my pistol are all in the gun room. I've gotten most of everything else cleaned and put away. Hey hon, where's your pistol?"

Joe took another swallow before saying, "It's in the prowler. I have another client coming in tomorrow I think. Aw shit, I need to look at my calendar." He walked into the gun room and called out, "Sweet, he's not going to be here until Saturday. I get to do absolutely nothing tomorrow. Oh, he can't ride so this will be an ATV hunt. Although I'll have two pack horses in camp. Jessie is bringing them up tomorrow. That way I don't have to pack one out if this guy gets one."

He sat down and cleaned and oiled both rifles and Kay's pistol. He walked back to the gun safe and put both rifles away and said, "Where do you want this pistol?"

Kay called out from the kitchen, "Put it back in the holster and in the closet by the door. Hey honey, do you want another beer?"

Joe smiled and slid six shells in the cylinder. He opened the door and put it in the holster. Leaving the hammer strap loose he closed the door and said, "It's in the closet and fully loaded. Yes to the beer." He opened the doors on the fireplace and threw in another piece of wood.

Then he finally dropped onto the couch and smiled as Kay walked in wearing shorts and a tank top. "Wow, you look comfortable," he said.

Kay smiled as she walked over, sitting on his lap and facing him. After one of those amazing kisses she said, "I took a shower and did a little yard trimming."

Smiling, Joe replied, "Mmm sounds inviting." Pushing her hair out of the way he started to kiss the back of her neck. Slowly working his way around to the side and back as Kay turned her head giving him full access.

Kay's eyes closed as she started enjoying the attention she was getting with the knowledge of what was going to happen next. Joe slowly stood up and lifted Kay in his arms as he walked to their bedroom and placed her on the bed.

He said, "Hold that thought. I need a shower." Laughing as he walks away he says, "Don't start without me."

Joe's internal alarm went off just a few minutes after five. Looking at the beautiful lady laying next to him, he reached over and put his arm around her and slid her across the bed. Kay rolled in his arms as that beautiful smile he loved so much came to her face as she said, "Good morning."

Joe smiled and replied, "Good morning. You were so good last night. I'm making you breakfast. What would you like?"

Kay smiled and responded, "Pancakes, sausage, and coffee. Oh, and the coffee first. I'll wait right here." She pulled the covers up and settled back into the pillow."

Joe had a surprise for her. While they were up hunting he had a carpenter come into their house and install a Kureg single cup coffee maker. It was behind a door on a roll away tray just above the little frigid they have in the bedroom. Less than two minutes later he walked back to a sleeping Kay with a fresh cup of steaming hot coffee.

Smiling, he whispered, "Hey, sunshine."

He placed it on the night stand and got the second cup already made. Sitting on the bed he slowly waved it back and forth until Kay started to wake up. Looking at the clock she says, "It's only been a few minutes. How did you do that so fast?" Joe pushed himself back and pointed,

"Every morning as soon as we wake up. Coffee can now be served."

Kay took another sip as the blanket fell away. Joe smiled as Kay said, "Maybe you should come back to bed."

An hour later Joe headed for the kitchen. A short time later he walked back into the bedroom with two plates of pancakes, sausage, and orange juice. Opening the sliding glass doors he called to Kay, "Breakfast is on the deck this morning." It was a beautiful fall morning with temperatures in the sixties. Kay walked out in her bathrobe and joined him.

Sitting down she reached for her coffee and took a sip before asking, "How many more hunters do you have this year?"

Joe replied, "Two this week and that's all. I'm hoping they both fill out quickly. I'm about done."

"I checked the website and there are already guys booking hunts for next year," replied Kay.

Joe looked at her and said, "Really. I knew it would grow quickly although I didn't expect this fast."

With breakfast done and cleaned up, Joe got dressed and headed for the barn. Getting his ASV he put two large bales of hay in the feeder and turned the horses out. Midnight exploded into a run. Kicking, bucking, and showing off. After a whirlwind trip around the paddock several times he finally settled down. He pranced around, his black coat glistening in the morning sun. Stopping, he looked at the house, hoping his human would be walking out. Then slowly he walked over and started to eat with the others.

Joe stood there watching when he felt a hand on his shoulder and said, "He's sure is pretty."

Kay smiled and said, "Yes, he is." Getting up on her tiptoes she kissed him and said, "Thank you again. I can't believe he's actually mine. I watch him everyday and love spending time working with him."

Midnight head came up as he scented Kay and watched as she approached the fence. Tossing his head he broke into that beautiful floating prance. After circling the paddock twice, he stopped directing in front of her. Then walked to the fence for the attention he knew Kay would give him and to spent as much time as possible between Kay and that other human he was forced to share her with.

Joe stood and watched as Kay patted and walked around with Midnight.

She started to walk and jog in a zigzag pattern. Midnight followed, her changing directions when she did. Joe drifted off as he watched them.

Joe saw Kay walk in from across the room. He couldn't believe how beautiful she was. Remembering the first time they met, he marveled at how the feelings he had for her stayed the same over the years. Kay had that smile too, the one that covered her face the first time they met for coffee. Joe remembered how he had lifted her chin for that first kiss and the way they melted into one another. Years later, the feeling they had every time their lips met was just as special as the first time they had kissed- even when Kay was in a hurry. It was as if the hurry ended when their lips met and the kiss took control. He smiled because he knew she loved him as much as he loved her. To him she was the world and more.

She walked back to Joe and climbed through the fence, interrupting Joe's thoughts. He jumped slightly as she said, "Come on, hon. Let's go and relax today. You'll be heading back into the mountains tomorrow and I want to spend every minute I can with you."

Standing there, they continued to watch as Midnight broke into his amazing prancing gate. Head and tail up, he made several laps around the paddock before finally slowing and walking to eat with the other three horses.

Kay reached over and took Joe's hand, giving him the slightest of tugs as he followed her hand-in-hand back to the house.

Kay slowly let Joe's hand fall as they entered the house. Joe opened the doors of the fireplace and asked, "How about a fire?" In a few minutes he had a fire burning and turned to see Kay standing there in a sheer black nightgown. Slowly, he stood and admired the beauty of the woman he was married to.

Joe took her hand and kissed her as he slowly walked her backwards towards the couch as Kay said, "Why didn't you build that fire in the bedroom?"

Joe replied, "Let's see if I can build a fire in you."

Kay slowly pushed him to arms length, giving her room to stand again. Taking him by the hand she led him to the bedroom. Kay turned and kissed him long and passionately as she started to take control. She walked him backwards and soon Joe was against the bed. Slowly, she continued to kiss him, getting closer and closer. Joe had no choice but to lay down on the bed as Kay continued to move forward, ending up on top of him. He reached for Kay's breast as she softly slapped him, and pushed his hands away.

"No, no," she said, continuing to kiss him and ever so slowly unsnapping his shirt. Slowly she slid her hands up and down his chest and stomach, easing down to kiss his chest. Again, Joe reached for her breast just to have Kay stop him and smiling as she said, "No."

She placed her palms on his upper arms and lowered herself to meet his lips. Kay slid her hand up, pushing Joe's arms and hands above his head. Slowly, she started to work her way down. Kissing and nibbling as she went. Stopping to softly suck on his nipples, she kissed her way back and forth across his chest.

Joe closed his eyes and relaxed as he enjoyed the reverse roles. Kay seldom became the dominant one. At the same time, she seldom, if ever, refused his advances. He could feel her hands as she slowly unbuckled his pants while she continued to kiss and nibble at his chest and stomach. Soon he could feel his pants as they slid away.

"Mmmmm," he moaned as Kay's hands found something new to entice her and torture him. She slowly caresses him. "Mmmmm," he moaned again.

She continued to play, kiss, and suck her way around from area to area.

Slowly, she worked her way up. Finding his lips, together they started that slow dance as their tongues found each other. Once again, Joe's hands started to slide down her back. As they started to move up to the front Kay caught them and once again she moved his hands up over his head. She sat up and moved her hips, feeling as Joe entered her with one quick push. In seconds they were in a perfectly timed motion. Kay had taken full control of what was happening. She could feel as Joe's motion changed and slowly she moved off of him. While still kissing and caressing his chest and softly sucking on his nipples. Joe's hands slid down as he slowly pulled her up and started to kiss her on the lips before slowly moving down to her neck.

As he reached for her breast again, Kay said softly, "No. Not yet." As she slowly slid his hands up.

Then she started moving and kissing her way down his chest and past his stomach. She kissed her way down the inside of his leg with her hand and found him. Slowly, she started to stroke him as she kissed her way back up the other leg. Her mouth moved to where her hand had been and the motions started again. Joe let out a long and low moan as she continued.

She could feel the tension in her husband melt away as his movements changed. Stopping again, she slowly kissed and caressed her way back up until she was laying on top of him. With one movement Kay was now on the bottom as Joe slowly settled his weight. Her legs slowly opened and slid up his side as Joe eased himself inside of her.

In a few seconds Kay was in perfect time. She loved the way Joe made her feel. He managed to reach deep inside of her and touch her heart. A place no man had ever touched before.

Joe had a wall built around his heart and managed to keep it there as a barrier for years. He was mostly scared he couldn't protect a woman from his past. Kay had torn down that wall in a matter of days and now they truly did live in each other's hearts. A place neither of them wanted anyone to ever get was now a place they both welcomed the other.

Kay felt the wave start to build. It built and built, rolling and curling, building higher and higher, until it broke into a body-shuddering crash. Her entire body shook as she released. As soon as that wave broke she felt another start. It rolled and built, rolling over and over, building higher and higher. She felt as Joe's movements increased and they shared one body-shuddering crash. Kay's breathing was still coming in gasps as Joe rolled onto his back, trying to catch his breath.

Slowly, Kay's breathing came back to normal as she rolled up on her elbow and asked, "Something to eat? Take a nap? Or..." she reached over and softly bit and then kissed Joe's neck. Joe rolled onto his side and slipped an arm around her. He replied, "I don't think I can do an encore performance right now. Although I am quite sure I'll be ready in an hour."

Kay giggled and said, "Come on, let's get something to eat and maybe watch a movie. I'm sure that fire you had going in the living room is nearly out. You fix it. I'll make lunch and we can talk about that encore performance you mentioned."

In a few minutes Joe and Kay were both up. Kay grabbed a silky black robe as she headed for the kitchen. Joe slipped on sweatpants and a T-shirt and headed for the living room. In a few minutes he had the fire going. Closing the doors, he headed into the kitchen to help Kay.

With lunch all done and cleaned up, they walked into the living room. Kay picked a movie and got it started as Joe placed a few more pieces of wood on the fire.

Walking back into the kitchen he grabbed two bottles of beer. Sitting down next to Kay and handed her one as he settled in to watch a movie.

The next two days flew past. Joe's first client had missed his flight and wanted to reschedule. Although with the season ending it didn't work out so he showed up a few days late and shot his bull the last afternoon. The last guy showed up a day early and by 4pm on the third day he filled his tag. With the season now over and a seventy-five percent success rate, Joe knew the business would grow. With the word now out and seventy five percent success. There would be an explosion of people wanting to book hunts.

Joe and Kay started getting everything cleaned up, repaired, replaced, and put away.

CHAPTER TWO

Joe stood and drank his coffee. He looked out of the window at the falling snow. He had already snowblown the driveway and the area in front of the large heated shop. Looking at Kay, he said, "I'm going to the shop to get the camper ready. As soon as it quits we are going to Arizona to get out of this snow and cold. I'm sure we have to work that gold chain some every year to hold it and we only have a couple of months left before the year is up."

Kay looked over her shoulder and asked, "Should I call Logan and Rene and see if they want to come with? I don't think there's much going on here until Spring."

Joe smiled and answered, "Yeah, it would be nice to get away from everything and everyone and spend a few months in the desert. Tell Logan to call me when he has a minute. Or maybe we should just run over there and see if they're interested in going?"

Kay smiled as she walked back to their bedroom to finish getting ready. Thirty minutes later they were sitting with Logan and Rene, talking about a gold chain and the warm weather in Arizona.

Logan looked at Rene and said, "This sounds just like what we need.

Some rest, relaxation, and fun for a few months. Before calving season and spring round-up starts along with everything else that happens at that time. I'm going to find either Jessie or Jerrod and let them know we are going to be gone for a while. They know what they have to do here."

Rene said, "I'll start packing what we will need from inside. You get what we need outside. Are we taking Star and Princess?"

Logan looked out the window and said, "Yes, it's time to start working with her and I think Arizona would make a great location."

Kay looked at Joe and asked, "How long before we leave?"

Joe looked at Logan then replied, "No big hurry. Say a few days?"

"That's good, just pack and when we're ready we'll go," said Logan.

Over the next few days Joe and Logan worked together getting Logan's camper packed with what the horses would need for a two or three month stay in the desert. They packed hay, grain, and the tack they would need for five horses.

Next came Joe's camper. Since they would be staying most nights in the campers, they wouldn't be needing all of the camping equipment. Although they would need mining equipment like shovels, picks, gold pans, climbing equipment, a small generator, pump, and gold sluice. They would also need the two side-by-side ATVs.

Playing for Joe always meant target practice so they also packed plenty of firepower. This time, it was in the way of six pistols and six more rifles. Two 9MMs, a .357, .44, plus two .22s. For rifles Joe grabbed two Remington model 700 in .22/250 and two AR15s, one in .223 and the other in .308. He also brought two Ruger 10/.22s along with a lot of ammunition for all of them.

With everything loaded, Joe and Kay were ready to leave. Joe went back to Logan's and checked to see if he could help them finish packing. Finding Logan in the shop he said, "I finished last night. I think I have everything that we will be needing packed. How about you? Do you need any help?"

Logan started to laugh and replied, "Nope, I've been ready. All I have left to do is load the horses."

Together they walked around the shop, putting a few things away and few more either in the trailer or truck. Then they closed the doors and walked to the house. Logan poured two cups of coffee as they sat down and went over the list again, making absolutely sure they had everything packed that they would possibly need.

Joe stood up and said, "Looks like we're ready to go." He glanced at Rene, looked back at Logan, then continued, "Let's be on the road by, let's say, six tomorrow morning."

Rene spun around laughing and said, "Six! What? Are you nuts?! Try nine, this is a vacation and relaxation time."

Joe laughed and walked to the door, stopping and saying, "I think I've kicked a hornet's nest here. You can deal with her, Logan. I'll head home and see if I can make Kay a very happy lady."

Snickering, Joe closed the door. Just as it swung shut, Rene yelled, "I'm calling her."

From outside, Joe called back with a laugh, "Hey, thanks. Ask if she needs anything and let me know." He walked to his Prowler and headed for home.

A few minutes later he was parking the prowler next to the trailer in the shop. With the pickup already hooked to the trailer, everything looked ready to go. Joe walked to the work bench, going over the checklist one more time to confirm they are ready to leave.

He walked inside and found kay. "Logan wants to leave around six tomorrow morning."

Kay started to laugh and replied, "Oh really? I just talked to Rene."

Joe smiled as he walked over and kissed her. "Opps. That may have been me."

Kay put her arms around him. Returning the kiss with a little more passion, she said, "Yeah, I think it's definitely you that wants to leave that early."

Joe gave her a hug and said, "I knew someone wanted to. I guess I just forgot who."

"Yeah. Now go clean up. Supper will be ready in ten minutes," she responded.

As they ate they talked about what they wanted to do in Arizona. Joe said, "I got a generator, pump, and small sluice along with other mining tools we'll be needing. Also Logan said he is bringing Princess. He wants to start working with her."

Kay replied, "That's great! I want to watch as much as I can. He did such a great job with CJ and Midnight."

Joe readily agreed and added, "Logan says CJ is very intelligent and caught on fast. The training of Princess will go fast if she's half as smart as him. Either way it will be fun to watch. He's simply amazing when it comes to training a horse and working with animals."

With supper over and the kitchen all cleaned up Joe headed for the living room, turning on some music and then starting a fire. Just as he sat down Kay came in with two cups of tea. They sat in silence and listened to the music and watched the fire.

Joe stood up and reached for Kay's hand as he led her to the middle of the floor. Turning, he put his arms around her and slowly they swayed in time to the music.

Kay looked into the eyes of the man she loved and said, "After all this time together you still do this. There are so many reasons why I love you and this is one of them. It's the little things you do." Going up on her tiptoes she kissed him long and deep. They continued dancing and kissing until the song was over. Then slowly they walked back to the sofa.

Finishing the tea Joe said, "Enjoy the fire. I'll make us two more cups." He grabbed both cups and walked into the kitchen, turning on the burner under the teapot he poured a flute of wine and walked into the master bath. After filling the tub with hot water he lit several candles and placed the wine on the edge of the tub. He then picked up the new book that arrived earlier that day. Looking at the cover he read, "*Deadly Desire*. She sure likes this trucking author."

Smiling, he thought, "I like his truck."

He fixed the tea and walked back into the living room, smiling as he looked into Kay's eyes. He handed her a cup and bent down, kissing her. Walking to the fireplace, he threw in a few more pieces of wood. He closed the screen and turned to sit down next to Kay.

They spoke about their new home and what they would want to do next when Kay said, "I'll be right back." As she headed towards the kitchen, Joe laughed and thought, *Yeah, in about an hour. When she sees that book I won't see her again unless I go sit in there with her.* Smiling, he finished his tea. Walking into the kitchen, he placed both cups in the sink. Grabbing another flute and the bottle he headed for the master bath.

Morning broke cold and windy as Joe sat up. He looked out the window and could see that it was still dark. Getting up, he walked to the sliding glass doors that went from their bedroom out onto a wrap-around deck.

He could see that it had snowed again during the night. Quietly, he got dressed and headed for the kitchen. After making a pot of coffee he then walked to the front door. Flipping on the outside light, he could see they had gotten nearly a foot of snow. He silently swore as he shut off the light and headed back into the kitchen.

After drinking nearly the entire pot of coffee he made another and got dressed. He headed outside to remove the snow from uncovered areas of the deck.

As he passed the sliding doors that led into the bedroom he saw the drapes were open and Kay was walking towards the kitchen. He quickly finished sweeping the deck and walked back inside.

Looking at Kay he said, "Another foot of snow again last night, maybe more. If Logan wants to leave today I'm sure we will have to put on chains to get over the pass out of here." Pausing, he looked out the window and said, "I'll call him after I get it cleaned up around here and find out if he needs help."

Joe slipped on his jacket and boots. Grabbing his gloves, he headed for the shop. He also grabbed a shovel and quickly moved the snow away from the doors, heading back inside. Starting his RT 75 ASV he drove across the shop and hooked up the seven-foot dual stage snow blower. Connecting the two hydraulic lines, he opened the door and attacked the freshly fallen snow. An hour later he had the area between the houses and the two garages all opened and so he headed for the barn. Walking inside, he fed and checked the horse's water, opening the doors so they could go outside if they wanted to.

He watched the horses as they ran and played in the snow. Getting in the ASV, he then made two passes down the mile-long driveway. Going back inside, he refueled the snowblower and called Logan.

Logan answered on the second ring and said, "Okay, you win. When do you want to leave? I've been plowing for three hours and I'm about halfway done."

Joe started to laugh and replied, "Not today, I don't want to chain up to get out of here. Besides, you're not done plowing."

Logan answered, "There's no doubt we would be chaining and you're right. By the time I'm done it will be dark."

"How's the road between your place and mine?" Joe asked.

Logan swore and said, "I tried and I can't push it. There are drifts in there that are four or five feet high and over twenty feet long."

Joe said, "I'll blow it open. If I'm not at your place in an hour, grab two pairs of snowshoes and come get me."

Logan looked at his watch as he started to laugh and said, "See you shortly." He disconnected and checked his watch one more time before starting to plow again.

Joe opened the shop door, stopping at the house. He told Kay, "I'm headed for Logan's. He's only about halfway done and is running out of room to push the snow."

On his way there, Joe found the first large drift that took nearly twenty minutes to chew his way through it. When he was nearly to Logan's, his cellphone rang.

Joe answered, "I'm not in trouble yet. These drifts are unbelievable. It took nearly twenty minutes to chew through the first one. I'll be in your driveway in fifteen minutes or so. Do you have coffee made?"

Logan replied, "Of course I have coffee. See you soon."

Joe and Logan sat together, drinking coffee and talking about what to do with all the snow. Joe questioned, "How about if I just start knocking them down and blow the snow straight forward?"

"Can you do that with ten foot high banks that have had time to freeze?"

Joe replied, "Sure, it just takes time and fuel."

Logan answered, "Then go knock yourself out. I'll plow everything to you and you can blow it out into the fields."

Four hours later they finally finished. Parking the plow and blower, they walked inside to have coffee and talk about the trip to Arizona. Grabbing the atlas and sitting on the counter, Logan said, "Let's take our time and see some country on the way." Opening the map, he continued, "Beartooth is closed for the rest of the winter. There's probably twenty feet of snow up there by now. Let's go this way." He dragged his finger across the map. "We might run into a little snow but it will be worth it. The Tetons are beautiful, plus we'll be going through the winter elk range by Jackson, Wyoming. Then we can head over here down through Flaming Gorge and south through Arches National Park, Zion National Park in the Moab Utah area."

Looking at Joe, he asked, "Have you ever been through that area?"

Joe replied, "Yes I have, although I'm sure Kay hasn't."

Logan said, "I asked Rene last night. She hasn't either. I know the girls will love it. We can do some riding or use your side-by-sides."

"That sounds like a great idea. I had better get home. I'm sure Kay will have dinner ready soon."

Logan said, "Pull over by the shop and I'll fill your tank before you head home. I'm sure you must be getting low by now."

As they were filling the tank Jessie walked up. Joe asked, "Hey, would you check on our house while we are gone?"

Jessie replied, "Absolutely, not a problem. Leave me keys and I'll check on the house and horses every day."

"That would be great, thanks." Looking at Logan, he continued, "I think I could have made it although I would hate to run out and try to get it running after dark." Turning, he thanked Jessie again. They stood there talking for a few minutes until the tank was full.

On the way back Joe had to reopen the road between his place and Logan's just to get home. He put the ASV and blower away, leaving it hooked up. Walking inside Kay said, "Rene called to thank you for helping. Logan says he's going to get one of those. He can't believe how far it blows snow and how good it works."

Joe replied, "I have a few other attachments that save me a lot of time around here. It really is handy. I'll talk to him while we are gone. I think we could share attachments, saving both of us money while having most everything that we need."

With dinner finished and everything cleaned up, Joe started a fire then headed for the shower.

Kay walked into the bedroom and asked, "Beer or tea tonight?"

Joe replied, "Let's have tea again tonight. I'm sure we'll have plenty of beer while in Arizona. I sure hope we can leave in the next couple of days."

They sat drinking their tea and watching the fire. Joe turned on the TV and found a movie they both would both enjoy. Getting up, he got two more cups of coffee. Then he threw a few more pieces of wood on the fire. He sat down next to Kay with his arm around her. She snuggled up against him with her head on his shoulder. Within minutes, they both fell asleep. Waking up just as the movie ended, he carefully picked her up and carried her to their bedroom. Laying her on the bed, he turned and walked back to the living room where he closed up the fireplace, put the cups in the sink, and locked the doors.

Walking back into the bedroom, he could see by the faint glow of the gas fireplace that Kay had managed to get under the covers. He stood there for a minute and just admired her. He couldn't believe what she meant to him and how much he loved her. He had honestly thought he could never love someone this much.

Getting undressed, he slipped in next to her to find her not only awake but also naked. Joe smiled as she rolled him over and started kissing him. *My god she is amazing*, he thought as he responded to her kisses.

Joe woke up to the smell of coffee and something else. *Bacon,* he thought as he came fully awake, *She's frying bacon.*

Getting up, he wandered into the kitchen. Kay turned, pouring his coffee as she walked to the table. Sitting across from him, she said, "Good morning, sleepy head." Joe glanced over at the clock. Shaking his head, he looked again. "Is it really seven?" he asked.

"Yes, it is. Rene called and said Logan would be ready before noon. If you weren't up by eight I was going to wake you," Kay replied.

Getting up, she finished cooking breakfast. As soon as they were done eating, Joe headed for the bedroom and the shower as Kay cleaned the kitchen. He quickly got dressed and loaded the two side-by-side ATVs and closed the rear door. Checking the list one more time, he opened the overhead doors, pulling the pickup and toy hauler out of the shop and parking it by the steps coming from the house.

He walked back inside and grabbed the cooler Kay had packed. Placing it on the back seat, he checked the heat, closing and locking the doors as they headed for Logan's.

As they pulled in, Rene walked up and said, "Logan's loading the horses now and we will be ready to go."

Joe got out and started to walk towards the barn just as Jessie emerged from the tack room. Changing directions Joe said, "Hey Jessie, I left the blower on it. I'm sure you can figure out how to run it. There's also a bale spike in the shop to lift those big bales. The water automatically fills. Just check and make sure the heaters are working. There's a new heater in the tack room. I also left five hundred dollars in there if you need anything."

Jessie said, "If you don't have it, we do. You can figure it out with Logan when you get back."

Joe responded, "Okay, then the five hundred dollars is for taking care of everything while we are gone. I can't thank you enough."

"Oh, that's not necessary," Jessie replied.

"Yes it is, so don't say anything and take it. I can leave without having to worry about anything here. It's worth it to me."

Looking at Logan Joe said, "Are you ready?"

Logan replied, "I just need to stop one more time."

Joe shook his head. "You've got to be kidding. What did you forget?"

Logan glanced at the house and said, "Rene."

Laughing, Joe turned and headed for his truck. Thumping the tires on the trailer, then on the pickup, he opened the driver's door to his wife with a huge smile.

Kay asked, "Are we ready to go?"

Joe laughed as he replied, "Yes, although Logan has to make one more stop."

"Oh my god. What did he forget?

"Rene." He laughed.

Kay started to laugh as she said, "Yeah, that is the one thing he probably should not forget."

Joe looked across the cab at Kay and said, "Nope, I'm sure we would hear her cursing a blue streak most the way to Arizona."

Kay watched as Rene ran out of the house and jumped into Logan's truck. She said, "We'd probably hear her a lot farther than just Arizona."

The mountain pass leaving Montana was snow covered and slippery. It required both of them to stop and put on tire chains. With the chains installed and also with four-wheel drive, they had very little trouble going up. Stopping at the summit, the guys quickly put on drag chains while Kay and Rene looked across the valley below.

The scene was absolutely amazing. A beautiful white carpet stretched across the valley to the mountains several miles away. With a ribbon of dark green, where the trees followed the course of the river through the valley. The gray of the cliffs mixed in with the evergreen of the pine forest as it filled in the mountain sides up to the snow-capped peaks.

Getting back inside, Joe said, "I put on a set of drag chains."

Kay asked, "What's a drag chain?"

Joe replied, "It's a tire chain that goes on the trailer tires. It keeps the brakes from locking and the tires sliding, keeping the trailer behind us. It's about six miles off this mountain and I want that trailer to stay back there."

CHAPTER THREE

Several hours later, in the shadows of the Tetons, they arrived in Jackson, Wyoming. They drove through town looking for a place to park for a few days.

They stopped at a convenient store and they both filled with fuel. While paying, Logan asked, "Do you know if there's a place we can stay? I have five horses with me. Two are studs although they are very well behaved."

The guy called out, "Hey! Does anyone know where someone with horses could stay for a few days?"

A guy walked up and said, "Yes, the animal barns at the fairgrounds are open. It's on the honor system. There's a sign that tells you what to do. There's also parking spots so you can park an RV there."

Paying the bill, Joe turned back and asked, "Could you please give me some directions?"

As soon as they arrived at the fairgrounds Logan looked around. Seeing an empty paddock, he turned CJ and Star loose while putting Joe's golden palomino Cheyenne and Midnight into a couple of stalls.

Joe carried in a bale of hay and asked, "Do you think we need another?"

Logan replied, "No, just one for now. Did you see where CJ and Star went?" He looked over as Joe finished feeding Cheyenne and Midnight.

"Yeah, Star and Princess are feeding by the corral. Although CJ is over at the neighbors."

"Ah, shit," replied Logan, dashing out of the barn. Joe locked the gate and followed him outside. Stopping, Logan scanned the area just to see CJ standing next to the coral with his head down. Walking towards him, he saw a young girl standing there petting his nose.

Logan walked up just as her mother came around the camper and ran towards her daughter. Logan called out, "Whoa! Slow down lady! He won't hurt her." She slowed to a walk but continued to approach CJ and her daughter.

The lady started petting the beautiful paint stallion as Logan walked up. Looking at the lady, he quietly asked, "Can she ride him?" The lady introduced herself, "Hi, I'm Tina. Is it safe?"

Looking at the young girls, he asked, "What's your name?"

"I'm Jordyn," she said. "He sure is pretty."

Glancing up then back at Jordyn, Logan asked, "Would you like to ride him?"

Jordyn's eyes glistened as she replied, "Really? I can ride him?" Looking at her mother, she asked, "Mom, is it okay?"

Tina looked at Logan and then at her daughter. She said, "I guess... this nice guy said you could."

Logan picked the girl up and put her on CJ's back. Pulling his head around he said, "Be good. No showing off." Pushing him away, CJ slowly started walking in a large circle.

Tina's husband, Sam, walked up holding his son's hand and asked, "Is he a stallion?"

"Yes he is," Logan responded. Looking at the young boy he asked, "Who's this young man?"

"This is Lee," Sam said.

Logan reached out and shook Sam's hand. To Lee, he said, "I am happy to meet you, Lee. I'm Logan."

Tina spun towards Logan with wide eyes and she asked, "Are you sure she's safe?"

Rene arrived and said, "Absolutely. She is safe. He is so well trained. He's been giving children rides for years."

Lee looked at his dad and asked, "Me too. Can I ride the black and white horse?"

Sam picked up his son. "Yes, you can. If it's okay with this guy."

"Yes you can, young man." Looking at CJ he commanded, "Over here." Then he added, "Slowly." CJ slowly turned and walked back to Logan. Stopping at his side just a few feet away.

Sam pet CJ's neck as Logan placed Lee on his back in front of his older sister. Patting CJ's neck he said, "Careful," as he pushed him away.

Star and Princess walked up looking for attention. Patting Star on the neck, he called Princess and said, "And this youngster is CJ's daughter, Princess." The young filly stood there as Sam and Tina scratched and pet her with Star standing next to Rene, watching.

While all this was going on, Joe and Kay climbed up on the corral and quietly watched. They had seen this many times and they were always amazed by how good Logan was with CJ and Star. It was like the two horses would do absolutely anything for him.

CJ walked in a large circle for twenty minutes while everyone pet Princess and Star.

Logan walked back to get his buggy whip. Arriving back to where everyone was standing, he called CJ over here-slowly.

With the whip standing against the fence, CJ walked up again, stopping just a few feet away. Logan reached up and lifted the two children down. He asked, "Would you like to see him in action? Maybe I should say get him to show off?" All four said yes.

Logan picked up the whip and walked about twenty feet away. CJ watched him go. Logan stopped and said, "Okay, over here buddy," as he cracked the whip.

CJ pranced away, circling Logan and stopping to face him ten feet away. Logan cracked the whip. He caught the whip end in his hand. He puts both hands up as CJ reared onto his hind legs, pawing the air. He walked forward and came down just a few feet from Logan. CJ then broke into a canter, circling and stopping again about ten feet away. Logan pointed right with the whip as CJ sidestepped to the right. Pointing left he sidestepped back. Logan dropped the end of the whip to the ground and CJ bowed to the small crowd that had gathered. Logan gave the whip a little snap and started turning as CJ broke into a high-stepping prance in a circle coming to a stop again and turning to face Logan. Then he turned away and bowed to the crowd with much applause.

CJ and Logan went through the entire routine with CJ bowing after every trick. Finally, Logan walked a short distance and leaned the whip against the fence. As he walked back towards the people that had gathered, CJ picked the whip up in his teeth and pranced up behind Logan, hitting him on the shoulder. Logan looked back and broke into a run with CJ behind him. The whip continuously hit him on the shoulder or on top of his hat.

Everyone in the crowd roared with laughter as the horse was now making the master do tricks. Logan ducked and dodge, cutting back and forth as CJ continued to chase him. Finally Logan was able to get back to where everyone was laughing and stopped. CJ walked up, dropping the whip. He bowed again and put his nose under Logan's arm. With nearly twenty people standing there the rides started again. Every young child that wanted to. They got a ride on either CJ or Star or both while Logan and Rene talked about the horses with their parents.

With the rides completed, Logan slipped a short lead rope from his back pocket. Hooking it to CJ's halter, he handed the other end to Star and said, "Go to bed." Star led CJ away towards the barn.

An hour later all five horses were in their stalls. The four friends were heading back into Jackson to have lunch and enjoy the sights.

As they drove through Jackson Joe saw a restaurant and asked the group, "Is anyone hungry?" Walking into the restaurant they saw a few of the people that were at the fairgrounds and had watched the show. They found a booth and listened as people talked about the black and white horse and the show they had seen.

When Jordyn and Lee spotted Logan they said, "Look daddy, there's the guy with the horses." Everyone turned as Logan and Rene, followed by Joe and Kay, walked in and sat down. People started asking questions about the horses. Either Logan or Rene answered most of them as the waitress took their order. Kay started reading the placemat and said, "Let's walk through the town square. We can look at the elk horn arches. Oh, and there's a sleigh ride that will take us through the Elk Refuge."

After lunch they headed towards the town square. While taking pictures of the elk horn arches, they read about the area's history and looked at pictures on history boards. They saw a sign that said sleigh rides and headed in that direction.

On the sleigh ride the tour guide talked about the National Elk Refuge. He spoke about the seventy mile migration from Yellowstone Park and that the migration had followed the same general route through the mountains for thousands of years. He said several thousand elk spent the winter on the refuge.

When the sleigh ride was over they headed back towards their campers. Joe stopped to buy several bundles of wood. As Kay and Rene started supper Joe built a fire and got the grill out to place over the fire. Logan walked up with four bottles of beer.

Joe and Logan talked about the trip to Arizona and the different places they planned on stopping. A few minutes later Rene and Kay walked out with four steaks. Joe used a small shovel to scoop hot coals out of the fire and place them under the grill. With the steaks sizzling, they continued to talk and enjoy the evening. The weather was pleasant, not overly cold, and the fire brought out a special feeling of warmth.

Joe looked over at Kay and said, "These steaks are nearly ready." Both Kay and Rene get up and headed inside to finish what they had been cooking in the camper. Soon, all four were outside eating steaks grilled over an open fire along with baked potatoes and green beans. Kay had fried some onions and mushrooms. In all it was a fantastic evening. Good friends. Good food. Good times.

The morning light started filtering into the camper when Joe sat down with his first cup of coffee. He heard his phone buzz as a text from Logan came in: *Are you up? Do you have the coffee made?*

Joe wrote back: *Of course I'm up and yes I have coffee made.*

Logan replied: *I've got some cinnamon rolls. Should I bring them?*

From Joe: *God yes. That sounds really good.*

Logan walked in just as Kay walked out in a sweat suit. "Good morning," Kay said as she took the cup of coffee Joe handed her. Sitting down she asked, "Is Rene up yet?"

Logan replied, "Yeah. She should be here anytime. She was just getting out of the shower when I texted Joe about the rolls."

Kay picked up her coffee and said, "I'll be back in a few minutes. I had better get dressed before she gets here. I'm sure she'll have plans to go do something."

Rene walked in and Kay handed her a cup of coffee and a cinnamon roll. As Joe and Logan moved to make a little more room. Logan said, "How do you like the rolls?"

"They are really good. Where did you get them?" Kay replied.

"What do you mean? I made them last night. After they were done I just left them on the counter overnight."

Kay shook her head. "Really, now, where did you get them? They are delicious."

Rene looked at Kay. "He made them last night. He made the dough just before dinner. Left it to raise while we were eating. Then as soon as we came inside he finished them before we went to bed."

"Oh my god," Kay exclaimed, "You have to be kidding me."

Rene answered, "No, really he did. I asked if I could help and he said 'Nope! just sit there and look pretty. I'll be done shortly.' After he finished he said, 'Now don't say a thing to them until after we have coffee in the morning.'"

Kay sat there not knowing what to say. There were so many things Logan could do. Although baking never entered her mind as a possibility.

Logan got up and said, "I'm going to let the horses out if there's no one here. Then I'm going to clean the stalls and feed them. I should be ready in an hour or so. I would like to go on the gondola ride to the top of the mountain."

Joe asked, "Do you want to hike to the top after that?"

"Nope. I'm on vacation. We are not hunting or running around helping people. So let's just ride the tram to the very top, have lunch, and ride back down."

Joe looked at Kay and then Rene. "Sounds good to me. It looks like there's a lot of snow up there."

Logan and Joe walked outside and headed towards the horses. Looking around he saw the gate on the corral was open. Walking inside he opened CJ's stall and lead him out into the corral. Joe had already closed the gate on the far end and was leading Star towards the corral also. Her little black and white baby was following closely behind.

With the three in the corral, Logan grabbed a wheelbarrow and pitchfork. In the matter of fifteen minutes he had the two stalls clean. Joe grabbed a bail of hay and put some in each of the four stalls. Joe led Cheyenne and Midnight out, turning them loose in the corral as Logan led CJ and Star followed closely by Princess back inside. The two studs had been together many times. Although in new surroundings Logan thought it was best to keep them apart.

They stood there watching as the horses ran around bucking, farting, and tossing the heads back. As soon as they had started to settle down, Joe grabbed both halters and led them back to their stalls.

Logan grabbed CJ and turned him back into the corral. Several people had stopped to watch the horses when Logan came walking out. He picked up the whip. Giving it a snap he walked into the center of the corral. CJ immediately started to prance around. Circling Logan he stopped to face him about ten feet away.

Logan looked at CJ and asked, "Do you want to put on a little show?"

CJ nodded his head and whinnied.

Logan put CJ through his routine. After each trick CJ would bow to the Audience, bringing more applause, laughter, and pointing. Everyone watching loved the show and CJ loved to show off. As the routine came to an end, Jordyn made her way to the fence. CJ walked up to her, lowering his head so she could pet his nose.

Logan walked over and saw Jordyn's parents. Stopping, he talked to them along with most everyone else that had a question. Nearly an hour later he put CJ back into his stall and walked back into the camper.

Pouring a cup of coffee, he joined the others. They were talking about the day's plans as they enjoyed their morning coffee and another fresh roll.

Joe remarked, "I think it's nearly an hour ride to get all the way to the top. If we leave now maybe we can get there and back by lunchtime. With the snow from last night I'm sure there will be a number of skiers looking to get up there also."

When they arrived at the top Rene's camera started clicking. She took pictures of the snow capped mountains above and the beauty of the valley below. The scenery was absolutely breathtaking. The black and white contrast of the rocks and snow mixed with the rich colors of the evergreen forest was majestic. Together, they walked around the summit and with every turn they found a view even more beautiful than what they had just seen. As Rene snapped picture after picture, Kay started talking into the recorder, taking notes for the article that they would write together at a later time. While Rene still worked for Montana Western Magazine, Kay was doing a little freelance writing for the magazine back in Chicago. They always tried not to write similar articles at the same time.

The ride up and back down was everything they expected and more. From the breathtaking views to the reactions of the other passengers.

Finding a restaurant, they filed inside for a late lunch and discussed how long they planned on staying. It was decided that they would leave the following day for the Flaming Gorge area of Wyoming and Utah.

Arriving back at the campers, they quickly fed the horses and then settled down around the fire to talk about where they would be heading next. Flaming Gorge and Dinosaur National Monument were definite possibilities. Both Logan and Joe knew they wanted to go through the Moab Utah area and Arches National Park. Little did they know the dangers that lay ahead in the deserts of Arizona.

With breakfast over, the camping area cleaned up, and the horses loaded, the four friends headed south with their next stop being the Flaming Gorge area of Wyoming and Utah.

With herds of elk and antelope on both sides of the highway along with the beauty from the Rocky Mountains, the trip through Wyoming was anything but boring. The mountains rose up to heights of over ten thousand feet. The sun reflected off of the snow and caused the rich deep green color of the evergreen pines to sparkle in the reflected light.

Rene and Kay talked continuously as they traveled south. With a camera snapping away and Kay talking into her recorder, they headed south on Highway 191 towards Rock Springs, Wyoming then on south through Flaming Gorge National Park and onto the town of Vernal, Utah.

CHAPTER FOUR

Finding a place to set up their small camp that they could also keep the horses at was the work of only a few minutes. A guy at a convenience store had two small corals just north of town. He told them it was free to use, they just needed to clean up after themselves.

Logan assured the man, "Thank you so very much. I promise the only thing we will leave will be tire tracks."

With camp all set up and the horses in the corrals Joe and Logan walked around collecting firewood. With an abundant supply of dead undergrowth it didn't take long to have a couple of evenings' supply. Joe dug around in the camper until he found what he was looking for. A piece of twenty-four inch steel pipe about a foot tall. Then he set up the grill that would be placed over the fire and slipped into notches cut into the rim of the fire ring.

As the sun sank from sight in the west it reflected back into the bottom of the clouds. The sky turned from red to pink to a lavender as the sun sank off the western horizon. The four friends sat and enjoyed a relaxing evening under a beautiful sunset in the high desert of northern Utah on the southern ridge of the Flaming Gorge.

Kay pointed at the far side of a small canyon as the shadows started to climb in. The way the sun was setting was bringing out the natural colors of the stone in the area. The canyon walls turned from a yellow-orange to a bright red. As the sun continued to set darkness overtook the area. Soon, the only illumination was just the fire light.

Logan and Rene got up while holding hands and walked over to check on the horses. Logan said, "I'll grab another bail of hay. Then I think we can leave them in the coral overnight."

To this Rene asked, "Are you sure Princess will be safe?"

"With Star watching her and CJ watching everything else I'm quite sure she'll be just fine," he assured her.

Walking back into camp, they sat back down at the fire. Kay had gotten marshmallows along with long sticks as her and Joe sat roasting marshmallows over the fire. Kay handed two sticks to Logan and Rene and asked, "Join us?"

Rene giggled as she replied, "Wow. I haven't done this in years," as she pushed a marshmallow onto her stick and started to roast it over the fire. Looking around she saw gram crackers and chocolate bars. "Mmmm," she said, as she pulled the hot roasted marshmallows off the stick between two gram crackers lined with pieces of milk chocolate.

With full stomachs the four friends finally said good night and headed for bed.

Joe sat straight up. Something or someone was moving around outside. Quickly, he dressed and grabbed a pistol and a tactical light. He walked out of the camper to see what it was making the noise. He could see the horses moving around uneasily. Soon he heard the snarl of a mountain lion answered by the defiant scream of CJ or Midnight, followed by the frightened whinny of Princess.

Logan came flying out of his camper screaming, "Damn cat is after Princess." He flashed his light around.

They could see CJ running around trying to stomp on something. Soon it was clear a mountain lion had tried to get Princess and CJ was having no part of that. There was absolutely no way a cat was going to get near his herd. With a crashing sound of splinter wood CJ had busted through the corral and was gone. Chasing a mountain lion away from his herd.

Two hours later Logan and Joe walked back into camp. They had been trying to find CJ to no avail. Dropping into a chair, Logan said, "I think I've walked fifty miles. I've looked most everywhere and I still can't find him. It's not like him to stay gone. He almost always comes straight back. I've whistled until my whistler doesn't work."

Joe looked over as Rene walked around the corner leading Princess followed by Star. Logan asked, "Is she or they alright?"

Rene replied, "Yes, they are fine. CJ scared the cat off before it could get to her."

Logan walked around, looking over and rubbing Princess down as he answered, "Thanks god for CJ or we may not have her anymore. Although I sure wish we could find him."

As they stood there talking, a bloody and battered black and white paint stallion walked into the fire light. Logan called out, "CJ's back!" The horse walked across the camp and put his nose under Logan's arm.

Logan stood there scratching his ears and patting his neck. With tears running down his cheeks, he said, "Am I ever happy to see you, boy." He started to rub him down while asking, "Where did he get you? These scratches don't look real bad. I'm sure they heal with a little care." Then he saw the bite in CJs neck. "Oh, shit. I think we are going to need a vet." Looking at Rene he said, "See if you can find a vet. He's been bitten here on the neck and there are some really deep scratches on his front shoulders. Look at these." He pointed at the deep gouges. "It looks like the cat was on his back."

Forty-five minutes later the vet arrived. Looking CJ over, he talked as he went to work, "I'll clean these up and stitch up a few of the deeper ones." Preparing a syringe of antibiotics, he handed it to Logan and said, "I just noticed he's a stud. Here, you give him this in a chest muscle. I've been bitten or kicked a few times too many times by these guys."

Logan looked at the vet and then at CJ and said, "Be good," as he patted his chest then stuck the inch and half long needle into it. CJ's chest muscle twitched as Logan pushed the plunger on the syringe. Withdrawing the needle, he patted him on the chest a few times then stroked the length of his neck.

CJ put his nose under Logan's arm as the vet gave him a shot of Novocain and started to close up the deeper cuts and gouges. Looking at the bite, he advised, "I'll clean this although it needs to be left open so it can heal from the bottom up and drain. Cat claws have terrible bacteria. I'll give you some antibiotic cream to keep it from getting infected. Also a neck bandage along with gauze to cover it and keep the flies out. From what I can see he'll make a full recovery." Standing up, he looked at Logan and said, "Can you tell me what happened?"

Logan looked at the beautiful paint stud. "Last night a mountain lion tried to get that little filly. This guy is her daddy and he didn't like that idea. So he chased the cat out of the coral then he broke it down and chased it clear out of the area. I have know idea what happened after he left here other than to say from the looks of him he more than likely killed it. Most of the time if a big cat gets on an animal's back it's a fight to the finish. As you can see CJ is alive and standing here. So I'm guessing that the cat is either dead or badly injured somewhere."

Logan handed Dr. Dan Stevens three hundred dollar bills. "You did a great job. Is this enough to cover the bill?"

Handing one back. Dan replied, "Let me see if I have change."

Logan insisted, "No, you keep it. You came not knowing us and I really appreciate that."

As Dan got his kit together he handed Logan a couple of syringes of antibiotics along with another neck wrap and some antibiotic cream to keep CJ's neck and gouges from getting infected.

Shaking hands, Dr. Dan headed back to town as Logan walked into the camper. Coming out with a rifle and pistol he stood the rifle against the camper and strapped the pistol around his waist. He declared, "I'm going to back trail CJ and see if I can find a wounded or dead cat."

"Wait a minute," Joe said, "I'll go with you." A few minutes later Joe walked out with a pistol belted around his waist and two rifles. Handing one to Kay, he said, "Keep this close." He looked at the coral where the horses were feeding.

Giving her a kiss, he said, "We should be back in a couple of hours. Looking at Logan he asked, "Are you ready? Let's go find that cat."

It took only a few minutes to saddle Midnight and Cheyenne. Logan swung up onto Midnight's back. Kay patted his neck and said, "You behave" before the two men rode away from the campers and back trailed CJ.

An hour later they found where the fight had taken place. Between Joe and Logan they found where the cat had jumped onto CJ's back. They could tell from the deep tracks in the desert sand what had taken place and where CJ had bucked and fought for his life. They could tell where he had finally gotten the cat off and where he had chased it into the bush and rocky canyons of the Flaming Gorge. As Joe followed the tracks, Logan looked up into the cliffs and tried to locate a wounded mountain lion. Joe found where the cat had tried to get CJ again and where CJ had chased the cat away by trying to stomp on it.

CJ was relentless in trying to find and kill the mountain lion. The trail of tracks and blood went nearly two miles down one valley up over the mountain side and into another.

Finally, they came to the area where the last battle had taken place. There lay a large male mountain lion, not the young juvenile they thought. This cat was in his prime, maybe five or six years old, and in perfect shape having lived on deer most of his life. As Joe walked up behind the cat, he nudged it with the rifle barrel. The cat moved and tried to spin around. Jumping back, Joe heard the crack of a rifle as Logan put the poor creature out of his misery.

Joe looked at Logan. "I have never seen a cat lay like that. He had to have heard us walking up?"

Logan watched as Joe rolled the large cat over and could see the damage CJ had inflicted on him: crushed and broken ribs, large areas of torn and missing skin where he had either been kicked or stuck by CJ's deadly front hooves, and two broken legs- one front one rear.

Logan pointed around the damage. "I'm thinking CJ hates lions. Look at his tail. It's broken."

Picking up the tail, Joe said, "It's been bitten. Look here." He pointed to the broken area. "You can see where I think CJ got close enough to bite him. It also looks like his back may have been broken also. That would explain why he laid here as we approached."

Logan looked at the back trail and said, "This is some rough country." Looking around, Logan continued, "He is half mustang, and for them, it's purely a fight to survive. With CJ still being a stud with all of those natural instincts plus the fact that he has fought off other cats, I think he's developed a natural hatred towards this poor guy." Pointing at the dead cat, he said, "Paid the ultimate price."

Joe and Logan both grabbed a rear leg and pulled it over by a large rock pile. Then together they started burying it, stacking a pile of rocks on top and around it. Once that was done they started the two hour ride back to the camp.

Once they arrived in camp both Kay and Rene listened as Joe and Logan unsaddled Midnight and Cheyenne. They then started telling the story of what they had found. Rene stood wide-eyed as Logan said, "At one point CJ had gotten close enough to bite and break the cat's tail."

As Logan finished telling the account of what they had found, Joe got up and walked into the camper. Coming out a few minutes later with four bottles of beer he handed two to Logan and opened and handed one to Kay. They stood there talking about what had happened and what they had figured out.

Logan turned and walked towards the corral. Leaning against it he said, "I'm so glad you came back," as he scratched and patted CJ's neck. Looking at Joe with tears in his eyes, he said, "I think I had better stop just turning him loose. I really don't know what I would do if he got seriously hurt. I've never had a horse I was this attached to."

Joe replied, "You can't put him in a stall and keep him there. He'll go nuts and you'll follow."

Looking at CJ, Logan nodded his head and said, "Yeah, you're probably right." Slapping Joe on the shoulder he said, "Let's go see what the women are up to."

Walking back to the campfire Rene met them with a couple bottles of beer. Sitting down the four friends stared into the fire and didn't say a word for several minutes when Kay broke the silence by saying, "I have supper nearly done. Would you like to eat out here or in the camper?"

Looking at Logan, Joe replied, "I've had enough outdoors for a while. Let's eat inside."

With supper finished and everything cleaned up, Logan walked to the corral to check the horses one more time. Joe joined him a minute later. As Logan walked around and between the horses Joe stared into the surrounding mountains.

Walking back, Logan asked, "See something?" He turned and looked.

Joe replied, "No, just looking." Smiling, they turned and walked back to the campfire. Logan picked up a couple of sticks of dried mesquite and tossed them onto the fire. Picking up his beer, he pulled a chair a little closer and sat down to relax.

Joe slid his and Kay's camp chair closer together and closer to the fire as she walked out with four more bottles. Handing them to Joe, he opened and handed one to Logan and Rene then one back to Kay as he opened the last for himself.

Talking about the day, the cat, and horses in a couple of hours the four friends headed for their campers for some much needed rest.

Joe stepped out of the shower and slipped on a sweat suit. Walking into the kitchen, he put water onto a boil as Kay headed for the shower. Twenty minutes later she walked into the kitchen wrapped in a towel.

Sitting down, Joe handed her a cup of tea. Taking a sip she asked, "How is CJ doing? Do you think we'll have any more trouble?"

Joe assured her, "CJ is doing great. A lot better than that cat. Oh, did I tell you it was an adult male? Weighing somewhere between one hundred eighty and two hundred pounds?"

Kay sipped her tea and her eyes snapped wide open. "That's about the size of the one that attacked us in the Bob Marshall a few years ago."

Taking a sip, Joe nodded his head and said, "Yes it was and that was a really big cat."

Joe reached over and flipped the music on, turning the volume down as they continued to talk about what the next couple of days could hold.

"I want to head south again in the next day or so. Arches National Park is absolutely amazing. If we spend a few days there then head for Arizona maybe we can spend some time around the Grand Canyon before heading for the Superstition Mountains and our," smiling and looking around he whispers, "gold claim."

Kay started to laugh and said, "Yes, be careful about who hears you." As she stood up and started to walk towards the bedroom part of the camper. Stopping just before the door, she looked back at Joe. With an evil seductive smile she let the towel slip to the floor.

Joe hurriedly put both cups in the sink and checked the door. He thought, *I don't want any intruders for the next couple of hours.*

As the sun started to peak over the eastern mountains, Joe was up drinking his first cup of coffee. He had rekindled the fire from the night before, then added a few larger pieces. In a matter of minutes he was alone with his thoughts. He enjoyed this time alone with his thoughts, his coffee, and a crackling fire.

A few minutes later Logan walked out and joined him. They sat looking at the fire and watched as the sky went from black to violet to rose then finally to a beautiful vivid blue. Still looking at the fire, Logan said, "Looks like a beautiful day is starting." Kay and Rene walked out at the same time. As they sat down Logan topped off their cups. Then looking at Joe, he asked, "When should we head south?"

Joe looked from Rene to Kay and replied, "Let's make sure this corral is good after our late night visitor and say we'll leave later today or first thing tomorrow morning. It's about three hundred miles to Arches then another three hundred on to Zion National Park and the canyonlands of Utah and Arizona. We could spend a couple of days in each either riding or using the ATVS. Then I would like to head for the Virgin River Canyon from Zion. We are only a hundred miles or so from there although I would like to get on the south side. I've driven through that area but never had time to actually look around. Maybe we can find a place to rent a canoe and float on part of the river."

"Wow that sounds great," said Rene. "Where is that located?"

Logan looked at Joe then said, "Utah, Arizona, and Nevada border. From what I've seen it's like a smaller version of the Grand Canyon. For wild life it'll be mule deer, desert big horns, mountain lions and rattlesnakes. Although the last two shouldn't be a problem. Snakes are pretty much all hibernating this time of year and the mountain lions have plenty of deer and sheep to feed on so they should stay clear of us."

Joe replied, "Next week should be a lot of fun and we'll see some really beautiful country. It's a little wild and rough but so rewarding."

In the matter of a couple of hours the corral was checked and fixed. Everything was picked up and put away. Anything that would burn was thrown on the fire. As all four walked around the area and gave it one more going over to make sure no litter was left, Joe dumped a couple of gallons of water on the fire. Then he made sure it was out and covered it with sand.

Walking over to Logan's camper he asked, "Are you ready to leave this little piece of heaven on earth?"

Logan looked across the canyon and said, "It sure is beautiful here. I'm sure I'll never forget this place." He opened the side inspection door and checked the horses one last time.

Joe nodded his head as he replied, "Yeah, I'm sure you won't. Well let's head south. So we can get to Arches Park before dark. I would much rather set up when we can see."

CHAPTER FIVE

Four and a half hours later they pulled into a camping area. After driving around they found a spot on the end with some grass for the horses. Logan parked and then Joe backed in at an angle to form an upside down V so they could put the horses in the center. In about an hour they had a camp set up and were enjoying a cold beer and watching the horses graze on the spring grass. Logan grabbed a bail of hay. That brought them all closer to where he was sitting.

Walking over he began to work with Princess. He was just petting her, rubbing her legs, picking up her feet for a few seconds. A couple of times she reached over and nibbled on his back pocket. She could smell something in his pocket that had her attention. He finally took out a couple of small carrots.

She taste tested them a couple of times before making both of them disappear. Patting her nose and scratching her ears, he walked back and sat down. Princess followed him, stopping at everyone and checking for more treats. Finally, she was rewarded for her efforts from Rene who produced a couple of apple slices. She nosed around for a few minutes, nibbling on Rene's finger and finally walking off to join her mother at the hay bail.

Rene and Kay got up and walked into Logan's camper. About twenty minutes later they came out with a light supper ready and the four of them enjoyed supper with Princess trying to taste test everything.

After supper Logan and Joe loaded all five back in the trailer and gave them all more hay. While Rene and Kay cleaned Joe started a fire and sat down to enjoy a quiet evening. The stars looked like they could be reached out and touched them. While sitting there talking and enjoying a beautiful evening, they watched as several meteors streaked across the night sky.

Shortly after eleven they headed for their campers and some much needed sleep. About three in the morning a thunderstorm blew in. Logan flipped the camera on to make sure everything was okay with the horses. After watching for a few minutes, he crawled back in with Rene and drifted once more to dream land. As morning broke it continued to rain and all four were stuck inside. Joe and Kay made a break for Logan's camper where they had coffee and breakfast until the rain let up late that afternoon.

The rain caused the desert to explode with color and by late that day you could see flowers of every color. The horses fed on the grass but never left the area around the trucks.

Joe started gathering firewood and Logan joined him after a few minutes. A large pile was stacked up next to the fire ring and Logan had a fire going.

Kay walked out with hamburgers ready to go on the grill while Rene warmed up beans and dished up potato salad. Soon they were eating, talking, and watching the horses. Princess had a little too much energy and did what young animals of every species do. She ran around like she was nuts. Kicking, bucking, and farting. Everyone laughed at her crazy attics. She tried to turn too fast and slipped in the mud. With her hooves going one way while her body wanting to go another, she ended up on her side. Finally, after several attempts to get up, she quietly walked back to eat beside her mother.

Logan walked over to check and make sure she was alright. Feeling her legs and scratching her ears, he also slid his hands down her back and sides. After fifteen to twenty minutes of petting and rubbing, he sat down with the rest and picked up his beer. Joe looked at the weather forecast and they started making plans for the following day.

As the morning light started to play across the desert, Logan and Joe saddled the four horses. Logan tightened up Princess's halter. He would allow her to run loose and follow Star as long as she stayed close. As soon as she got too rambunctious he would attach a lead rope and then she would be forced to stay close.

Princess was a little angel the first day. Never getting more than twenty or thirty feet from her mother. If she did fall behind, she would catch up by running as fast as she could, flying past them, circling out wide and settling in alongside Star. This caused a little excitement the first couple of times as CJ and Midnight both loved to run. They would immediately start to prance and side step because both wanted to run with her. One time when she came flying up behind them Logan turned CJ loose followed seconds later as Midnight exploded in a neck-and-neck race with CJ. The two stallions flew across the desert. They had huge hearts and lungs of a quarter horse, combined with the stamina of a mountain mustang, matched against the natural stamina of the Arabian stallion who had been bred to run for thousands of years. It was quite the match as the two horses raced neck-and-neck. The race was short lived as the power and explosive start of CJ and Midnight became instantly visible. In a few powerful strides both horses were at full speed and gaining fast. Princess heard and felt them coming up behind her and turned on the speed. Both horses flew into action as they came up alongside her. One on both sides they started cutting her off and turning her back towards the others.

As they rode through and around Arches National Park, Rene's camera snapped continuously and Kay talked into her voice recorder about the natural wonders they saw. Late that evening they headed back, arriving at the campsite about two hours before dark. In the matter of thirty minutes Kay and Logan had the horses rubbed down and fed. While Joe had a fire going and Rene had dinner nearly ready.

With dinner done and everything cleaned up, the four friends sat by the fire and enjoyed a beer, light conversation, and looking into the beauty of the desert sunset. The sky showed a color scape that went from amber to rose to violet to finally a beautiful dark purple hue all across the horizon. The color changed with the distance to the horizon as the sun reflected its natural beauty on the clouds.

Logan and Joe got up and checked on the horses one last time. Standing next to the fire with Kay and Rene, they looked into the desert night as a coyote yipped his defiance to the world. Putting his arm around Kay, they said good night and retired for a few hours of privacy.

Morning broke absolutely crystal clear. As the sun rose, so did Logan. Making coffee, he filled his cup with a craft. Checking on the horses he settled down to enjoy the peace and quiet. Joe came walking up from the little river they were camped by. Logan reached over and filled his cup. Looking around he asked, "Where were you?"

Joe glanced back over his shoulder and said, "Just walked down to the creek and checked out the area close around here. There are trout in that creek. It must flow year-round or maybe they just come up here when it is flowing."

Logan laughed as he replied, "I thought I may have woken before you. I looked around trying to see if you were sitting out here by the fire. So I checked the horses and then sat here waiting for you and the girls."

Joe took a sip of coffee and asked, "So what are the plans for today?"

Logan looked around and said, "Not sure, maybe we should take the wheelers and go play for a while. Pack a cooler with lunch and water, maybe a few beers, and explore?"

Joe started to laugh as he asked, "Are we in a hurry?"

Logan glanced over his shoulder and said, "I don't see the girls yet. So I'm guessing no."

Joe snickered and said, "That's good. I'll get the wheelers out. I'm sure when I start them the girls should wake up."

From behind Joe, Kay said, "I'm already awake, up, and moving. I heard Logan say something about packing a cooler so I started getting one ready. Give me twenty minutes and I'll be ready to go."

From the other camper Rene called out, "Yeah me too. I can have another one ready in about the same time."

True to their word, the two girls were ready in an hour as Logan placed one cooler in the back of each wheeler. While Joe checked the wheelers, topping off the gas tanks, then strapping two five gallon cans in the back of each, they were off for a day of exploring.

Logan checked the horses one more time making sure they had hay and water along with double checking to make sure the fans were blowing through the trailer.

Joe punched a few buttons on the GPS and they were off to start exploring the area. A little over an hour later they stopped on a high plateau overlooking a huge canyon.

Logan pointed and asked, "What's that moving down there?"

Joe tossed him a pair of binoculars. As Logan focused on the area he saw movement. "It's a herd of desert big horns."

Joe picked up the other pair and said, "Wow. Desert big horns. They are endangered now. We are lucky to see them. I was out here several years back to help trap several for science. They took blood samples, got their weights, put them on radio collars and turned them loose. They are one stout animal and can go months with little or no water. And talk about strength! They are one solid muscle. From nose to tail."

Moving closer to the rim, they stood and watched as the small band of desert big horns moved out of sight. Looking at the others Joe said, "Do you want to follow them? There is a very good possibility we could see more?"

Rene put her camera down and replied, "I'm up for that. I would love to get a few more pictures."

Looking at the other two Joe replied, "Ok follow me."

He headed for a path up a little rise and along the rim. Coming to a point where the path started down Joe froze as Logan said, "Is that a rattlesnake?"

Joe replied, "Yeah," as he started looking around expecting to see a western diamondback or maybe sidewinder. When he said, "Everyone look around very carefully, there's a yellow rattler just a few feet in front of me. They are yellow in color and have a faded diamond pattern. If you see one say something and stay way." Slowly, everyone started moving back up the hill. Joe found a long stick and carefully picked the rattler up. The snake slipped from the stick and started moving towards him. Striking several times, he tried again to pick it up. As they moved backwards, the snake continued to follow them. Joe finally got the stick under it and moved it off the path. With it moved out of reach and off the path he told the others, "The venom in this guy is more deadly than that of the Cobra and they have no problem injecting up to fifty percent of their storage in a single bite. They are one of the deadliest snakes in America." Carefully, he slipped the snake back into a crack in the rocks as they looked for another trail to follow the sheep.

Logan asked, "Where did you learn about that snake? I've been in this area several times and never ever heard of a yellow rattler?"

"I had a job removing rattle snakes from a housing development north of Phoenix," he explained. "I had several in a cooler and stopped to talk with the guy that hired me. I showed him what I had caught that day. When he saw the yellow one he quickly shut the cooler and said. "'Do me a favor and kill that yellow one.The rest are just rattlers. Although that yellow one is absolutely deadly. When I got about thirty miles out in the middle of nowhere, I opened the cooler. That snake came over the side and actually chased me. I ended up killing it although I didn't want to. I picked it up three times and carried it about twenty feet away. It came back like it was tracking me. The rest just crawled away. Not that yellow one. They are just too aggressive. I caught snakes in that area for a week and found several of those yellow ones. They all acted the same. That's the only time I've actually looked for them. I really didn't enjoy it, other than that one trip where I spent years working with and rescuing wildlife. Plus the fact I've spent the majority of my life wandering around in the mountains and desserts."

Joe watched where he had put the snake to make sure it stayed there. Finding another trail, they continued to follow the sheep and took pictures.

Kay walked up next to Joe. Slipping her hand into his, she said, "Every day you amaze me with your knowledge of the outdoors. When I think about what you know plus the fact of what you have done, there are times it actually scares me. Why haven't you been seriously hurt by the animals you work with?"

Putting his arm around her then looking into her eyes he replied, "I'm always as careful as I can be. Although I have been hurt a couple of times, like that damn bear in Alaska a few years ago. I also had a mountain lion attack me once. I managed to get a hold of a club and smacked it a few times to change its mind. Plus there have been many other close calls. Like that grizzly in Montana when we first met."

Kay turned and looked at him saying, "You said he wasn't looking to cause us any trouble."

Joe smiled. "He was way too close and a lot closer than I wanted him or any grizzly to be when you are with."

Joe kept looking up into the mountains when he saw a light reflecting flash. Glancing at Kay who was looking down into the valley below, then at Logan who was looking directly at him, Joe calmly said, "Let's head back. It's getting late and I really don't want to be hiking in this area after dark."

Logan reached for where his pistol should have been to instead find an empty belt. Looking from Rene to Kay and finally to Joe he said, "That sounds like a great idea." He gave Joe a *What the hell was that?* look.

Just shy of an hour later and before dark they got back to where the two wildcats were parked. Pushing a couple of buttons on the GPS, Joe called to Logan saying, "It's about ten miles to where we are camped."

Logan replied, "Lead on. I'll simply follow you."

Joe reached, checked Kay's seatbelt, and hit the starter. In a few minutes they were speeding across the desert and headed towards their camp.

Upon arriving at camp Joe immediately went in the camper and picked up his H and K .45. Working the action he slipped it in the small of his back and went to start a fire. Then he filled both gas tanks as Kay went in to start supper. Logan headed for his pickup, grabbing his Colt 1911 .45 checking to make sure it was loaded. He slipped it back into the holster and clipped it to his belt. Finding Rene, they headed for the horses to check on them making sure they had hay and water.

Joe headed towards the camper just as Kay walked out with four nice ribeye steaks. Turning, he grabbed the grill. Then he pushed the logs around to calm down the flame and dropped in a few pieces of green mesquite. Placing the grill on top of the fire ring he put the steaks on and sat down next to Kay, opening a couple bottles of beer.

Logan and Rene came walking up. Logan grabbed two more beers, opening them he handed one to Rene and dropped into a camp chair saying, "Now that was a fantastic day. Seeing those sheep was great. Although I don't care if I ever see another of those snakes."

Kay came walking out asking, "How long on the steaks? Most everything in the camper will be ready in ten minutes."

Rene replied, "What can I do to help? I went with Logan to check on the horses."

Logan picked up the fork and turned the two in the center as Joe said, "These should be done about the same time. I tossed a couple of pieces of mesquite in there tonight. It burns hot and the smoke should give the steaks a slightly different flavor." Then gave Logan a wide eyed look. As if to say I have know idea what that was earlier.

Logan glanced up into the surrounding mountains and back at Joe to wordlessly tell him that he had seen something also.

Joe got up and reached for the fork to turn the steaks again. As he did, his shirt came up slightly and Kay asked, "Why do you have a pistol clipped to the inside of your jeans?"

Joe stood up and moved his hand to where the gun was and said, "Wow, I'm so used to having one I forgot it was there." Then pausing for a few seconds he continued, "Okay, fine. While we were following the goats just after seeing the snake, I saw a light reflection up in the mountains. I'm sure it wasn't anything, but after what happened a few years ago, I feel better if I have it."

Logan said, "I saw it also. From now on I'll have one with me at all times." Reaching up, he touched his neck where the bullet had grazed him a few years earlier and said, "I really don't want to go through anything like that again. Maybe we should all carry one. Just as a safety precaution."

Kay looked from Rene to Logan and then locked eyes with Joe. "Light reflection? As in a rifle scope?"

Joe held his wife's gaze and said, "I'm not totally sure. Although maybe tomorrow we should find a new place to camp for a few days. Say twenty to thirty miles from here."

CHAPTER SIX

Javier arrived back into camp with a huge smile. Looking around he asked, "Where are Hector and Juan?"

Carlos said, "They should be down by the jeeps. The guy just got here to take possession of our cargo."

"That's great," Javier answered. "I really want to get headed back, although I think both Hector and Jain are going to want to stay."

Carlos turned and walked back to him saying, "Why would they want to stay. What did you find?"

Javier connected the laptop to his camera. "Only this," he said as he opened a program and showed Carlos pictures of Kay and Rene standing on a cliff edge looking into the valley below.

Carlos said, "Oh shit, here we go again. Were there two guys with them?"

Javier replied, "Yes, there were two gringos with them. Although I'm sure we can kill them. I've seen pictures of those ladies in Hector's and Juan's personal duffle bags. I know Juan has offered a large amount of money to anyone that can bring this one to him." He pointed at a picture of Rene.

Carlos replied, "Yes, and I'm quite sure Hector would give you whatever you asked for if you brought him the other one. I still think both of them are nuts. Sure, both of those women are beautiful, but come on. They nearly died trying to take them away from those two gringos last time. Plus last year we were in Montana and that guy named Joe scared the shit out of all of us. One night he snuck around and tied up all of our look outs without ever being seen or heard. The following morning Hector absolutely freaked. He made us leave right then and there."

Javier looked at him. "Wow, really? I know Hector from Columbia. Although that was a long time ago. I was just a nobody while he was in close contact with the cartels. That's where he met Juan and started this. I helped load the cargo to be shipped here." Looking around he continued," While in Columbia say about ten years ago there was a guy that caused so much trouble for the cartels they put a two million US dollar price on him. There were a few guys that survived a meeting with him. They said he was like a ghost. They never heard or saw a thing and suddenly they were trying to find a place to hide. He popped up only meters away and started shooting. All the cartels figured out it was him and not a different cartel causing all the trouble. So they put several hunting parties together. He killed most of them before one finally caught him. They tortured him for a couple of days before he escaped killing several in the process. They tracked him to the American Embassy in Bogota. In the last few minutes of a gun fight he killed several more before running through the Embassy gates. The guards opened up and killed most everyone else. Out of twenty guys only three lived to tell what happened. That gringo is just like him."

Carlos asked, "What happened to the gringo in Columbia?"

Javier replied, "From what I heard he was all shot to shit. They think he died. It was reported that he had been hit several times. Although we don't know for sure.

Carlos looked around. "I can tell you this. You show those pictures to Hector and Juan and we won't be headed back to Mexico anytime soon."

Javier looked at the pictures for a long minute. Closing the laptop, he looked at a picture of his wife and said, "Let me think about this. Maybe it would be best to let the past stay in the past and just get back to Mexico." Picking up his equipment, he headed for the main camp and supper.

Carlos watched as he walked away. Closing his eyes he quietly said, "I feel a fight about to start. Those two gringos are not going to like us trying to take their ladies again. I know I would protect María." Slowly, he stood up and followed Javier to the camp.

Hector and Juan walked towards Javier as he approached, saying, "Did you see anything?"

Carlos froze at the question and thought, "Oh, please don't tell them!"

Javier replied, "Not really. Just some hikers but they are not coming this way. They were in the bottom of that far northwest canyon."

Carlos smiled as he walked to get something to eat. He thought, *Thank you. I just want to go home. We don't need any trouble now. We've delivered our cargo. Let's just get back to Mexico.*

Hector looked at Juan and then to Javier and said, "I wish we had more time. I would like to go to Montana and get Kay. Then just turn and run like hell for Mexico."

Juan said, "If you do, make sure you grab Rene also."

"Why would I grab Rene? You want her, you go get her. It's bad enough having Joe chasing me. I don't want to piss that damn cowboy off too."

Javier looked at his laptop and then over at Carlos. Pausing for a minute, he picked everything up and walked to his tent. Putting everything away, he laid down on his sleeping bag. He closed his eyes and drifted off.

Carlos slowly walked over and sat down until he finished his meal. Throwing the last couple of bites into the fire, he walked to his tent thinking, *I just know he's going to say something and shit, we'll be running all over trying to find them. I've got to talk to Santiago. Maybe he can convince those two idiots to leave and go home.* Laying down, he closed his eyes and slowly drifted away.

Morning broke cool and clear as Carlos crawled out of his tent and started looking for Santiago. Finding him talking with Hector and Juan, he hung back and poured a cup of coffee. Sitting down at a table, he watched out of the corner of his eye until he walked away. Getting up he called out, "Hey, Santiago wait," as he quickly walked over, handing him a cup of coffee, he looked around and quietly said, "Kay and Rene are in the area. Javier saw them yesterday. He has pictures and if he tells Hector or Juan we'll be chasing them all over again. What do you think we should do?"

Santiago rubbed his forehead and said, "Aww, shit. That's all we need. We are still in the US. We can't start that here. We'll all end up in prison. I had better talk with him and convince him to stay quiet before he gets a chance to talk to Hector and Juan."

Carlos opened his laptop and said, "Look what I found."

Turning the screen so Santiago could see, he continued, "It seems Joe and Kay West have a gold claim east of here in the Superstition Mountains."

Santiago finished reading and said, "Well at least we know where they are headed. That'll make finding them again a little easier."

"If I get close enough I can put a tracking dot on one or both of their trucks. That way we can find them most anywhere and anytime we want."

Santiago said, "That's a great idea. Give it a try but make sure you don't get caught," as he turned and headed across the camp in search of Javier. Seeing him standing by the small creek, he walked up and said, "I heard you got a couple of very important pictures yesterday. Now listen if you show them to those two idiots we'll be chasing them all over the place. I'm going to have Carlos track them and report back to me where they go. When the time is right I'll tell you. Then and only then can you tell Hector and Juan. If they give you a reward it's all yours. You get all the credit."

Javier looked around and said, "I don't want either of them mad at me. Juan isn't playing with a full deck. He is liable to shoot first then ask what happened."

Santiago replied, "I'll take care of Juan and back you. I hate that man like I've never hated someone. I would love nothing better than to simply put a bullet in his stupid ass. Although he has the money. So please just do what I say. Besides, I think I know where they are going. There's a place in the Superstition Mountains. When we are closer to the border we can start this. You can show them the pictures and I'll tell you where they are so you can lead us to them."

Javier looked around and saw Hector. He said, "Okay, but if he figures out that I've had this information and these pictures he'll go nuts. He could just shoot me in a fit of rage."

Santiago replied, "I'll back you by saying we wanted to make sure it was them."

Javier watched as Hector walked towards them saying, "Alright," as he then walked away.

Hector called out, "Hey Javier, where are you going?"

Javier turned and said, "Finding some food and coffee."

Hector looked at Santiago and said, "Where is Carlos? I've been looking for him."

Santiago replied, "I put him on lookout today. He left an hour ago."

Hector looked like he was about to explode as he screamed, "Why?! You know we are leaving this morning. Everything is complete and we need to get back across the border as soon as we can."

Santiago stepped back. "Sorry, although we still need to have lookouts watching to make sure US law enforcement isn't watching us. He's going to report to me and follow us out. Watch our back trail and catch up when we get close to the border."

Hector stood there scratching his head and said, "Okay. I knew putting you in charge would be a good idea." He turned and walked to where Juan was standing.

Santiago stood there and watched as Hector and Juan started talking. Hector turned and pointed at Santiago as Juan yelled, "I'm in charge! Everything has to be okayed with me and go through me. I don't want that Columbian idiot out there just wandering around where he could get caught."

Hector poked his finger into Juan's chest and said, "You are in charge of getting the product from Columbia to us. I'm in charge of getting it to our people in the US. This is a fifty-fifty arrangement. Now, on the way back we are going to find a couple of cute college girls. Between the Asians and Colombians we will have a really fat payday. So back off and relax."

With that, Hector turned and walked away, leaving Juan standing there alone about to explode all over the place. Looking at Santiago, he walked towards him saying, "I want to talk to you."

Santiago replied, "Make it quick. I have to make sure everything and everyone is packed and ready to go. We have about three hundred miles before we are safely back across the border."

Santiago walked away and left Juan standing by himself as his temper continued towards the boiling point. Turning, he stomped back towards the main camp and started yelling orders which brought Hector at a much faster pace. With Juan nearly ready to blow his top, Hector grabbed him and said, "You need to shut up. We know what we are doing. Each and every guy here has done this before and they don't need to be looking around to make sure you're not about to explode and start shooting the place up. So just shut up, sit down and relax."

As he turned to walk away, Juan followed him, still yelling, "This was my deal! I'm the one in charge! You take orders from me. I won't have you telling me what to do."

Hector stopped and slowly turned around. Looking at Juan he said, "Let's walk over there. Away from all the men. They don't need to hear you acting like a total fool."

Juan looked where Hector was pointing and replied, "No, I think not. I'm going to watch and make sure everything is done to my liking. Then we can leave."

With an argument over Hector saw Santiago. Walking to him he said, "Get everything packed as soon as possible. Let's head back so we can get rid of that idiot. He gives me one hell of a headache. I want to get rid of him and he'll never be coming with us again."

Thirty miles away with the sun behind him, Carlos watches as Joe and Logan start breaking camp. With everything loaded Kay walked out of their camper. She was wearing a sundress that left very little to the imagination.

He continued to watch them break camp and he thought, *How can that gringo drive with her sitting just a few feet away looking like that?*

Kay headed for the other camper just as Rene walked out in a tank top and really short shorts. Carlos zoomed the scope a little better and readjusted. He thought, "I can definitely see why Hector and Juan want these two. I think I want them too."

From his vantage point he could see that everything was nearly ready to go. Looking at the road, he figured there was only one way out and they'd pass the same road he came in on. Grabbing his equipment, he headed for the Jeep and the trail back down the mountain.

Finding a low spot, he climbed to the top of a small hill and waited for them to pass. He figured they were about five miles away and watched as they drove past. With them ahead he ran for the Jeep and started to follow, staying back far enough that he could barely see them.

As they hit the interstate, he hung back several cars and continued to follow. An hour later they exited the highway and pulled in to get fuel. Carlos pulled up the gas island and topped off the Jeep. Watching he saw Joe and Logan fill their tanks and the girls go inside. A few minutes later he was rewarded as Joe and Logan followed them inside.

Grabbing a couple of tracking dots, he walked past the campers and stopped to tie his shoe. Carefully Carlos placed the magnetic dot on the inside of the rear bumper on each pickup. Walking inside, he quickly paid for his gas and went back to the Jeep. Opening the laptop, he brought up both GPS dots and typed the names for both as he watched them leave the parking lot. Now he could access their location from anywhere, nearly immediately by simply pushing a few buttons on his laptop.

Pulling the Jeep into a parking spot, he sat back and relaxed, closing his eyes. He was ready to take a much needed nap. He knew he could find them at any time and most anywhere.

An hour later Carlos picked up his phone and called Santiago saying,

"It was a complete success. I've got those GPS dots on both pickups. We should be able to locate them wherever they are twenty-four hours a day."

Santiago replied, "That's great. Hector and Juan have been fighting all day. I'm about to put both of them

 out of our misery. I can't stand either one anymore. Juan is just a complete ass and Hector isn't much better. I think you had better get back with us as soon as you can. Do you have a location on us?"

Carlos opened the laptop and said, "Yes, you are about sixty miles from me moving southeast. I'll catch you sometime later tonight or tomorrow. I'll keep checking your location so I'll know where and when you stop tonight. The route you're taking through the mountains will slow you down. I'm alone and so I can go around. I'll see you tomorrow morning."

The following morning Carlos drove into camp. Seeing Santiago, he said "I checked their whereabouts and they are still headed towards south eastern Arizona. At this point I'm quite sure they are headed for that claim."

Santiago replied, "Just keep checking on them. Tell me when they stop and spend more than ten hours. I'm sure you are right."

Just then, Juan started shouting orders again saying, "Hurry up! Let's get moving! We are spending way too much time sitting around. We need to hurry and get back across the border."

Hector walked out and said, "Just slow down. Don't hurry. We have to look like we are on vacation. If we go flying across here we'll draw too much attention." Then turning to Juan he said, "You need to shut up. I've been doing this for ten years. As long as we look like we are relaxing and maybe prospecting the law will leave us alone. Now just stop barking orders. These guys know what they are doing. We've yet to have any trouble with law enforcement. So shut the hell up."

Seeing Carlos, Hector walked that way and asked, "Did you see anything? Are we being followed?"

"Nope, not a soul out here," Carlos answered. "Our back trail is clear and I checked up ahead also. Everything looks good."

Turning to Juan, Hector said, "All clear both ahead and behind so just relax. I know what I'm doing."

As day turned to night the gang of drug running slime balls camped in a small canyon off the main road a few miles. It was a place they had camped several times before. This trip had taken them farther into Arizona than they had ever gone before. Usually they met their contact south of Phoenix. But that area was getting too much attention so they moved their meeting location a hundred miles north. This was safer for the contacts but made it much harder on Hector and his gang of human trash.

As the sun started to rise in the eastern sky, Hector and his gang started to move. With coffee brewing and breakfast cooking everyone started to pack again. As soon as they were done eating it was time to go. Santiago walked over to Carlos and asked, "Where are they this morning?"

Carlos opened his laptop and replied, "Wow, about twenty miles north of us still heading in an easterly direction."

Santiago opened a map and followed the road that Joe and Logan were taking. He said, "If they keep going the way they are they'll end up in the Superstition Mountains."

Carlos hit a few keys and logged into the state mineral website and said, "Here's his claim information. It only shows a rough location. He hasn't worked on it much and has about a month or so until the claim is invalid." Looking at Santiago, he continued, "Maybe we should make a detour and check that out, watch them for a few days and if it looks like they are finding gold we could rob them or better yet ambush them. Hopefully, we can kill the two guys and get those two ladies. Juan and Hector would pay us dearly for them. Although I think maybe we should keep them for ourselves first."

They thought of Kay and Rene standing there talking the day before, wearing only shorts and tank tops. He closed his eyes and could picture them both naked and tied in such a way he could just walk over and pleasure himself with each for a few days. Then he could turn them over to get the reward being offered.

Smiling, he said, "Those two are really good looking. I'm quite sure they could make a guy very happy." He rubbed his crotch and laughed, added, "And man would I like to be happy."

Santiago smiled. "Let's figure out a plan and find a few more willing to take the risk. We can separate ourselves from the rest after we have everything set."

With a plan starting to take place, Carlos kept track of where Joe and Logan were headed while Santiago thought about who he could trust and who would be willing to fight. He knew Joe and Logan wouldn't willingly hand over the two beautiful ladies. He also had to outmaneuver Hector and the nut chase Juan. As long as those two kept fighting that part would be a lot easier.

Javier walked up to Santiago and asked, "When are we going to show Hector and Juan what I saw a couple of days ago?"

Santiago explained, "As soon as they calm down. Right now if we bring that up they either kill each other or one of us. I want you to go out on patrol this afternoon after we stop. When you get back you can tell them. They are camped about 20 miles east of us." He paused for a minute, then continued, "Maybe I should go with. That way there are two of us to confirm the story. Neither Juan or Hector would think it was made up if we both said the same thing."

Shortly after the caravan stopped for the day to continue their exploration of the desert, Santiago and Javier left to sit stake out. After finding a spot high on the mountainside, the pair sat down to start going over the plan that Santiago and Carlos had carefully put together. Javier wasn't too impressed with the idea and said, "That doesn't sound too smart to me. Juan has a habit of simply killing everyone that crosses him and Hector likes that damn knife. I think he actually enjoys torturing people."

As they sat on the mountainside Santiago continued to try and convince Javier that the plan would work and he should throw it in with them, although it was becoming painfully clear. Javier was scared of the two leaders.

Santiago stood and said, "I'm going to walk down the ridge and see if there's a place we can get to the desert floor. I want to get closer to where Joe and Logan are camped."

CHAPTER SEVEN

Under the cover of darkness he made his way toward the small fire he could see. He knew what was there and wanted a closer look. Crawling the last two hundred yards, he laid quietly and watched as the four Americans prepared supper while enjoying each other's company. He watched as Kay and Rene walked back and forth in the fire light. He could see the light dancing off their clothing. He could also see as the light passed through Kay's sundress and what lay underneath.

Quietly, he slid a little closer. The sight of the firelight passing through that sundress was overwhelming and he wanted a closer look. When he got within twenty yards he was just out of the light ring circling the fire and he stopped. With a couple of bushes covering him he lay down and started to think about what he wanted to do to both of them- but mostly Kay. As she walked around cleaning up and putting things away she passed between the fire and where he was lying several times. With each passing, Santiago could feel himself getting more and more excited. Closing his eyes he thought, "I will have her. I must have her."

With everything cleaned up and put away, the four friends settled down to enjoy the fire and one last beer before calling it a night. Santiago continued to watch and listen, trying to pick up any parts or pieces of the conversation that drifted to him. He heard words like gold, climbing, and work but nothing he could put into a complete sentence. Although he knew that with the tracking dots they could find them most anywhere they went.

After an hour of hiding behind a clump of mesquite brush and spying on the four friends, he carefully backed out and went to find Javier. He knew that convincing him was going to be a hard feat. He was scared to death of Hector and Juan. Although, as of now, he was the only one that knew anything about the plan that hadn't joined the group.

He slowly made his way away from the camp as he heard one of the horses snort and then nicker. Freezing in place, he saw Logan stand up and walk over to check and make sure everything was okay. CJ nickered again as he approached and looked out across the desert.

Logan pats his neck and said, "What's out there boy? What did you see?" Standing only fifty feet away, Santiago slowly lowered himself to the desert floor. Listening, he could hear Logan talking to the horses.

With CJ calmed down, Logan checked on the rest, stopping and patting each of them on the neck, then running his hands over their backs. With everything looking to be okay, he turned and headed back to the camp.

Santiago let out a long slow breath. *That was way too close,* he thought as he crawled away. Standing up, he headed back towards where he left Javier.

Javier climbed back up to where he was sitting. The two guys stood there looking at the camp below when Santiago said, "I think we really need to get those two women for ourselves. I have a contact that would pay us."

Javier looked at him. "What about Hector and Juan?"

Santiago replied, "Screw them, we can split the money four ways. That's about two hundred thousand each. I'm sure they would bring about four hundred thousand on the Asian market. Women like that are hard to find and bring really high prices in Asia."

"Yeah, maybe," replied Javier. "Although Hector and Juan would kill us if we did something like that."

Santiago looked at the camp again. Lifting his binoculars, he said, "Kay is standing next to the camper. Looks like she's had a nightgown on. I would absolutely love to spend a couple of days with her before selling her."

Lifting his binoculars, Javier looked and said, "Oh my god, she is beautiful. Yeah I would too. I'd give a month's pay to have her for a week."

"Yeah, and Rene is nearly as beautiful as her. Just think about having both whenever you want for a week or two. Then split the money from the sale."

Looking around, Javier said, "Why don't me and you just go down there. Kill those two gringos and take the women?"

Santiago replied, "Hector and Juan already tried that. Those two gringos didn't like that idea and fought like hell to keep them." Pausing, he looked around and said, "It'll take more than just you and me. I have a couple others that'll join us. Then we can take them. Let's keep following them and when the time is right we'll get the women and kill the two gringos."

Getting up, they started the hike back to camp. Santiago said, "Now get rid of those pictures you have. I don't want either Juan or Hector to see them. Also, don't say a word about this to anyone. I'm the only one who knows who's all in this and I'll say when we go."

Javier looked at him pointedly. "So you really do have this set up?"

"Absolutely," he answered, "and if we do this right, we'll all be rich men and can quit this caravan crap and stop making Hector and Juan rich."

Arriving back in camp, Javier walked into his tent. Getting out his laptop, he opened the files and emailed the two pictures to himself. Then he deleted them from the picture file and they were off his computer. He now only had one copy in his phone.

Next, he found Carlos and said, "I talked to Santiago. He's nuts. He's going to get us all killed."

Carlos replied, "Keep this quiet. We can't let anyone find out or you'll be the first to know what it's like when that idiot Juan just starts killing everything and everyone."

Carlos stood up quickly when he heard shouting coming from just south of the camp. Sitting down, he said, "Oh my god, Hector and Juan are at it again. I wish one would just kill the other. Listening to them all day and half the night is sickening."

Javier stood up and said, "I have ear plugs in the tent. I'm going to sleep. Besides, I think I walked fifty miles today around," pausing, he slowly looked around and continued, "you know who." Laughing he headed towards his tent.

Carlos got up a few minutes later and saw Santiago walking across the camp. He jogged to catch up and said, "Looks like you got everything set up. All we need is to have one of those two idiots kill the other and everything will just fall into place."

Santiago stopped in front of his tent, looking around. He replied, "That's too much to even hope for," smiling, he continued, "although it would be a dream come true."

Turning, he opened the flap and headed for bed.

CHAPTER EIGHT

As the morning light started to filter through the shades on the camper, Joe was up and making coffee. A few minutes later he stepped out of the shower. He quietly dressed, filled a travel mug, and stepped out into the clean fresh air. Gabbing a camp chair, he pulled it closer to the fire. Picking up a stick, he pushed the coals around, adding some smaller sticks and in a few minutes he threw in a few bigger pieces.

Sitting there sipping his coffee, he enjoyed the warmth of the fire. He heard Logan's camper door open. Looking over, he saw Logan headed his way with a cup and craft of coffee. Logan offered to fill his mug again and sat down.

Joe said, "Morning, dude. Did you get any sleep? Kay and I could hear you two half the night."

Logan replied, "Yeah, she gets a little loud sometimes. Especially when-" The camper door opened.

"Especially when what, Logan?!" Rene yelled out.

Logan smiled and got up, grabbing a camp chair. Putting it next to him, he then filled her cup and said, "Good morning. Here, sit down and relax. I'm sure you are still tired after last night. I know I am."

Kay walked out of the camper and laughed. "Yeah, so am I. You two need to either quiet down or park your camper farther away."

Joe started to laugh as he tossed another piece of wood into the fire. Logan asked, "Now, how far is it to your-" looking around, he whispered, "gold claim?"

Joe chuckled and said, "There's a road that cuts through the desert about thirty miles from here. After we hit that it's about forty miles. There's a small town just a few miles from the claim. I think we can stay in town tonight. Check all of our equipment tomorrow morning. Stop at the hardware store and get whatever else we might need and I think we'll head for the claim after that. I want to try and find my way through the underground tunnel. It'll make bringing in this stuff a lot easier. I also want all of the climbing gear in there just in case. Kay and I got lucky when we found a way out. I don't want to try that again. My chest still hurts. I won't say what it did to her."

Kay reached over and punched Joe's shoulder. "You made it all feel better. I didn't mind at all."

Logan chuckled as Rene said, "Maybe we should go in that way. Then we can listen to you two."

Kay replied, "You would have heard us if you two weren't so busy."

Joe started to laugh as he got up. "Come on, let's get packed and head for town. We can finish this conversation tonight over a couple of cold beers. There's a nice little bar there."

Logan let the horses out and cleaned up the trailer. After feeding them, he caught Princess and hooked a lead rope as he started working with her. Making her walk in a circle around him, then trot in a circle, and finally gallop. After that he gave her a rub down, a bucket of water, and put her in with Star. With the horses all loaded and everything picked up, they walked through the camp area one more time, picking up anything that doesn't belong.

Looking at Logan, Joe called out, "Hey! Are you ready?"

Logan answered, "Yeah, as soon as I find Rene."

Rene called out, "Hey Logan! Joe! Come here, you need to look at this."

Logan walked to his wife and looked at where she was pointing. Joe walked up, looking down then around he took a few steps. He slipped his hand under his jacket and wrapped his hand around the grip of his pistol. "We had a visitor last night."

Joe pointed to another set of tracks and said, "Those are mine. I walked through here yesterday morning." Following the trail backwards, he said, "Here's where he laid down and watched us." Turning, Joe followed the tracks and saw another place where he had laid down in the sand. Looking at Logan he said, "He laid here also."

Logan replied, "CJ was looking this way last night when I checked on them. I looked out here but didn't see anything."

"That was after dark. There's no way you could have seen anything. Although CJ's eyes are much better than yours after dark. Not to mention his smell. He may have seen someone but you can bet he smelt him."

Logan said, "That's it, come on, let's get out of here. I think we had better stay in town for a couple of days and keep our eyes open and mouths shut. Let's see what we can find out before going to your claim."

Looking at Logan, Joe replied, "Yeah, I think you're right. Let's go."

With everything picked up loaded up, the two pickups headed southeast for a little town in the desert of southeast Arizona. As soon as they were moving, Logan said, "I want you to carry a pistol at all times. And if need be, use it. I have a bad feeling that it may be Hector and his group of human slime balls again. I'm not taking any chances. I could be wrong, I just don't think so. I'm sure Joe is telling Kay the same thing."

Arriving in Silver Springs, they filled both pickups and all the gas cans. They also put gas in the two-wheelers and generators. Next they asked around for a place to stay with horses. A guy at the convenience store said, "You can stay at the rodeo grounds. There's a barn with stalls and it's all lit up at night. No one will mess with you there plus it has a good well. There's a box mounted on the wall by the office. It's on a donation system. So just pay what you can. Here's my number. I'm Jim Stevens. I own the feed store in town. If you need anything, call. I'll have someone deliver it to you."

Logan put the number in his phone and thanked the man. Looking out the window at the trailer, he continued, "Could you deliver, say, thirty bales of hay and a couple fifty pound bags of horse feed? Do you have the kind with molasses plus grown corn and oats?"

"Absolutely," said Jim, "It'll be there this afternoon."

Logan looked around and asked, "Where did Joe and Kay go?"

"They went to find a restaurant. Kay said she would text me what they found and where they are."

"Have you heard from her?"

Rene replied, "Don't know, my phone is in the truck. I just figured I'd check as soon as we are done here."

A block away at Donna's Diner, Joe and Kay had just sat down. Kay reached for her phone, looked up, and froze. Her eyes were open wide and she started to shake. Joe looked at her and saw sheer terror in her eyes. He knew there was only one person that could cause that kind of a look in her. All Kay could do was stare and shake.

Joe's left hand slowly went inside his coat. He couldn't remember if he worked the action and put a shell in the chamber or not. Slowly, he looked over his shoulder. Standing fifteen feet away were two men he hated.

The dinner was nearly full. With people standing all around he knew he couldn't shoot. Letting go of the pistol, he picked up the two steak knives and waited. With his back towards them and the blades of the knives against his arm he started to stand. Turning, Hector spotted him and his hand started to move towards what Joe was sure was a gun under his light jacket.

Joe's left hand snapped as a steak knife flipped through the air to nearly disappear high in the right side of Hector's chest. Pablo looked from Hector to Joe as the other knife glanced off his cheek leaving a deep cut in his cheek. Joe charged the two men and in a diving tackle all three went through the plate glass window.

Now standing just a hundred feet away, Logan turned to the shouts of people trying to get out of the way and the sound of breaking glass to see Joe and two other guys come crashing through the store front and land in the street.

Logan started running towards the crowd of people that had gathered outside the diner. He saw one guy pointing a pistol. Logan hit him from behind just as he pulled the trigger. The crowd scattered from the gunshot. Leaving only Joe who now stood facing Pablo. Joe's left fist connected solid with his chin as his right hand grabbed a handful of hair. Pulling his head down while bringing his knee up into Pablo's face. He broke his nose and sprayed blood down his neck and chest and all over Joe's pant leg.

Logan grabbed hold of the man with the gun, driving his fist into the man's face and knocking him against the wall. His eyes rolled up as he slid down the wall out cold. Turning, he saw a couple more of Hector's gang starting towards Joe. Logan stepped in and blocked their way. Grabbing one by the throat, he lifted him from the ground. Hooking his other hand between the man's legs, he body slammed him into the wooden walkway. Turning just in time to see Joe drive a left into the others face and a hard right into his solar plexus.

With the fight in the street getting everyone's attention, Rene slipped into the diner. Grabbing Kay, they went out the back door and ran for the pickups.

Arriving at the camper, Kay grabbed two 9MM semi-automatic pistols. Checking to make sure they were both fully loaded, she ran back towards her husband and the free for all. Looking back, she saw Rene only a step or two behind her with a short barrel shotgun. Kay heard as Rene worked the shotguns action, loading it while still running back to help their husbands.

Running into the center, Rene saw two men holding Logan as one continued to pound away, hitting him several times. Lifting the shotgun, she saw Joe on the ground being kicked over and over by the two others. Touching the trigger she sent a blast into the air, working the action and pointing the barrel at the three guys now standing just a few feet from Logan. Out of the corner of her eye she could see Kay holding both guns on the guys by Joe as he slowly got to his feet and tried to close his torn and ripped shirt. Turning back, she watched as Logan walked over and picked up his cowboy hat. With the hat in his left hand, he drew back and let loose with a hard right, connecting with the man's chin that had been hitting him just a few minutes before, sending him crashing into the others as all three fell to the ground. Then taking the shotgun from Rene he turned to face the rest of the gang of human trafficking drug running scum saying, "I hope a few of you think you're sneaky enough to get to your gun. It'll give me great pleasure in killing you."

Pablo elbowed Hector and said, "Did you see the scars on that guy's chest? If he's who I think he is, then I put them there about twenty years ago. I'm sure he recognizes me. He's had some very good work done, but I'm sure it's him. He's the ghost of Columbia. He's worth at least a million US dollars in Columbia. We need to get him. We can just kill the other guy later and sell the women."

Joe started to slowly get to his feet. He rubbed his ribs before taking one quick step and spinning, kicking one of the guys in the side of the head. He knocked him off his feet and landed face-first onto the tar road. Then stepping to the side, he snapped and kicked the other, catching him under the chin. The man was thrown backwards, landing on his shoulders. The two men struggled for a couple of seconds before falling back and laying still.

Joe walked to Kay as she handed him her left hand gun. Just as the guy tried to get up, Joe walked over and slammed the butt of the pistol into the back of his skull and watched as he dropped once more to the ground.

With Logan and Kay standing guard, he walked up to Hector. Grabbing the knife, he gave it a quick twist before pulling it out. Hector screamed in pain as Joe said, "I can't believe it. You are on the US side of the border." Looking around, he pointed at a lady and said, "Call the state police or sheriff's department. Whoever is closer. All of these guys are wanted and it's time for them to pay for all they have done."

Santiago and Javier came running up from behind. Pointing their fully automatic rifles in the air, they both let loose with a short burst. As everyone in the crowd froze, they pointed them at Logan and Joe as Santiago said, "Don't be stupid. Just let them slip to the ground. Carlos, help Hector. Let's go before the law shows up and we have to fight our way out of here."

Javier walked over and grabbed Rene's arm. Just as Logan let loose, a bone crushing weight connected with solid, sending him crashing into Santiago. Hector tried to get to his feet with help from Pablo on one side and Carlos on the other. Carlos let Hector go and fired a short burst into the air. Getting everyone's attention, he yelled, "Enough! You cowboy go over there or I'll put a bullet in your knee. Javier, get up and help Hector. Just leave her for now. Santiago, clear the way out." Carlos reached over and grabbed Rene by the hair and gave her a hard yank as he pointed his rifle at Logan and said, "Bye cowboy, she's my whore now. I'll be screwing your wife good and hard in an hour."

Logan looked at Joe and then to the ground where their guns were laying. Joe turned his arm just a little so Logan could see the knife he had just pulled out from Hector's shoulder. With a snap of his wrist, the knife suddenly appeared, sticking out of Carlo's neck with blood spraying everywhere. Carlos squeezed the trigger, sending a balance magazine into the air. Rene saw Kay and jerked free as she ran in that direction. Carlos clutched his throat and sunk to the ground.

The shots from Carlos caused what was left of the crowd to scatter in every direction. While Santiago tried to figure out what had just happened, Logan and Joe both dove for their guns. Now armed, they came up and fired, sending a few more of the human trafficking scumb to meet Satan.

Looking around, Joe saw Kay and Rene kneeling behind a nearby car and he started to run in their direction. Now with the two ladies behind him, he looked for Logan. With people running in every direction, he watched as Logan tried to get a shot through the fleeing crowd at the retreating group of human waste. With no shot possible through the crowd of people Logan stood up, walked to Carlos, and stood guard as he waited for the medical personnel and law enforcement to arrive.

Joe looked at the two women and said, "I'll be over by Logan." Looking around and back at the two women he continued, "Are either of you armed?"

Rene held up her pistol. "Yeah I am. I managed to grab it in the confusion."

"Good I'll be right back." He nodded and walked off.

Approaching Logan, he said, "Both of the girls are right behind that car." He pointed to where they were both kneeling.Looking back at Logan, he asked, "Is law enforcement on their way? To be honest, I would rather this ass just die here."

Carlos's eyes opened wide as he held the knife sticking in his throat. He gasped, "You can't kill me. There are witnesses."

Joe replied, "If I turn that knife just a little you'll bleed out right here and now. So it's best you just shut up and pray I don't."

Both men snapped around as they heard a scream and several gunshots. Looking, he saw Kay laying on the ground a few feet from the Jeep they were hiding behind. Taking aim, Joe emptied his pistol at the back of the Jeep as it sped away. Turning, he ran to Kay and helped her to her feet.

"What the hell just happened?" Logan asked.

Through sobs and tears Kay replied, "There were two guys hiding in that Jeep. As soon as all the commotion started they jumped out, knocking me down and grabbing Rene. I tried to get a shot as I was falling but I missed. By the time I got into a sitting position the door was closed and the car was moving. Oh my god, they have Rene. Joe, they have Rene. What are we going to do?"

Looking around Logan asked, "Is there an airport where we can get a plane? If we hurry, maybe we can find them?"

"I'm sure there's an airport," said Joe, "but by the time I go through all the requirements they'll be in Mexico. We need something now."

CHAPTER NINE

Arriving back at camp, Hector screamed, "Where are they?! We need to know if they are following and where they are. Where's Carlos? Hey Carlos, where are you?! Has anyone seen Carlos? We need to get into his laptop and see where they are."

Javier walked up holding Rene by the arm and declared, "We have this one and she's mine."

Juan looked across the camp. Getting up, he walked over and grabbed Rene's arm, jerking her away from Javier and saying, "Wrong. She is mine." Reaching behind his back, he pulled a pistol and shot Javier in the chest. Everyone reached for their guns not knowing where the shot came from.

Pablo raised his pistol and screamed, "Enough! Now everyone calm down." Pointing his gun at two of the guys he said, "You and you. Take his body and dump it out in the desert."

Santiago looked at Diego and said, "Shouldn't we bury him?

"No! Just dump him. He doesn't deserve to be buried. He's too stupid.

Everyone knows that she's mine." He jerked Rene in front of him. Continuing he said, "Now where the hell is Carlos?"

Santiago replied, "Carlos was captured in town. That damn Joe had a knife. He threw it and stuck it in Carlos's neck. I saw him fall as we were trying to get you two out of there. I'm not sure if he's dead or not. Although there sure was a lot of blood. I looked again as we ran past. He was just laying there with that knife sticking out."

Pablo pointed at Javier and said, "Would someone please get this dead body the hell out of here? Now, where is Carlos's computer? We need to get into it. We have to find out where they are."

Diego came walking up with Carlos's computer. Opening it, he hit a couple of keys and said, "It's password protected."

Hector screamed, "What do you mean password protected?! Why would he do that?"

Diego replied, "Wow, this is tough. It looks like if we get it wrong it'll delete everything and there's no way to get in without the password."

Hector asked, "Does anyone know what Carlos would use for a password? We need his computer. Or we break camp right now and make a run for the border. I'm sure by now every cop in Arizona plus Joe and that damn cowboy are hunting us. You know what that means- we have to split up. As soon as we junction with the canyon trail it's every team for themselves. We'll meet back in Mexico at the mission village." Pausing, he looked around and said, "Now does anyone have an idea on a damn password?"

Esteban called out, "How about his wife's name. I think it's Maria?"

"Or maybe his daughter Elena," suggested another.

"His father's name was Cesar," someone else called.

Juan stepped up, slammed the laptop closed, and said, "We are wasting time. Let's just go and if we keep moving it'll be hard for them to locate us."

Everyone stood there waiting for Hector to say something. Juan pointed his pistol at Diego and pulled the trigger. The larger caliber bullet hit him high in the shoulder, blowing him over backwards. Picking up the computer, he walked to Santiago and said, "Work on this. Hopefully you can get it to open."

Hector screamed, "What the hell are you doing!? We sure as hell needed Diego. He knows this country almost as well as Carlos. You stupid asshole! Now we will need to stay together. We are short two of our best chances to get back to Mexico safely."

Juan replied, "It's easy. Mexico is south so now we just go south and in a few hours we are in Mexico."

Hector shook his head. "Oh, really? What about all the sensors that the border patrol has placed all over? Diego and Carlos knew where they were. They could have guided us through that area. Now we have to hope we don't draw too much attention to ourselves. They also knew the patrol times. So now we also have to watch that we don't run into one of them."

Juan turned and said, "Mario knows the way through. I think we should take the chance and simply follow him."

Alejandro called out, "He's new. He hasn't proven himself. How do we know he won't just lead us into a trap? Just because he's your friend doesn't prove anything to me. I don't trust you, let alone him."

Juan yelled, "All I know is that if we want to get back to Mexico we'll need to move soon!"

Santiago replied, "Yeah, he is right. Break camp now. Five guys to a Jeep. Be ready to move in twenty minutes."

Thirty minutes later Hector was helped to a Jeep by Pablo and Juan. As he got into the front seat he reached out and grabbed Rene's arm, pulling her close he whispered, "You are going to bring a great price after Juan is tired of fucking you. I think I'll keep you for a few weeks. Then maybe bring you to boy's town in Tijuana. You'll make a lot of money for me there. Then I'll put you on the Asian market." Juan pushed her into the back seat and handcuffed her to the door handle. Rene jerked against the door handle several times. Juan finally had enough of her jerking and swearing and backhanded her hard across the face. With Hector and Pablo in the front, they left without looking to see if everyone else was ready. Quickly, the rest fell in. Hector didn't really care if the rest got caught or not. He knew the route through the desert that would lead them safely back across the border.

Santiago pulled in line and looked over at Pedro. He said, "If I get half a chance I'm going to kill that ass. I really liked Javier and Diego."

Pedro sighed and said, "If I get home I'm done. It just isn't worth it. Spending time in an American prison doesn't scare me as much as Juan. He's nuts."

CHAPTER TEN

Logan saw the feed store owner walking across the street. Reaching in his pocket, he grabbed the piece of paper, took a quick glance and called out, "Hey Jim! Hey Jim Stevens! Wait a second," as he ran towards him.

Jim stopped and looked around as Logan ran up and said, "I need a place to leave five horses. Two are studs. They are very friendly and will behave although they are still studs and I want them to stay that way. I'll call my ranch and have a couple of my guys leave right away although it'll take a couple of days for them to get here. My wife was taken in that street fight and Joe has two wild cats. We are going after them and her."

Jim responded instantly. "Yes, I can take them. I have a small ranch just a mile or so out of town. Let me get my pickup and I'll meet you here in ten minutes and take you out there."

Logan asked if they could leave their trucks and trailers there too. Together, the two men ran back to where Joe and Kay were standing as Logan finished explaining what was going on.

In a matter of minutes after arriving Logan and Kay had the horses in separate stalls in Jim's barn. Standing next to CJ, Logan stoked the neck of the beautiful black and white stallion cooing, "You be good. Jessie and Jerrold will be here in a couple of days to take you home. I need to find Rene. I'm sorry boy but this time you cannot come. I'm sure there's going to be a bad fight to get her back and I don't want to take a chance on you getting hurt." Pausing, he looked at the beautiful paint stud through tear-filled eyes and thought, *I've never been this attached to a horse. It hurts to leave him but it'll be far worse to lose Rene.* Stroking CJ's neck a few more times he dried his eyes and looked towards Kay who is doing pretty much the same thing with Midnight.

She stroked his neck and said, "You be good- I'll see you at home in a few weeks." She then turned and followed Logan out of the barn towards a waiting Joe.

Fifteen minutes later Joe strapped two five gallon gas cans in the back of each of the wild cats. Then he strapped two more cans to each of them. Shaking Jim's hand, he looked at Kay one more time and said, "I really want you to stay here and go home with Jessie and Jerrod."

Kay snapped around and replied, "That's not happening. I'm going. Rene is my best friend and I'm going." With her belt already buckled on she slid a full magazine home, snapped the release and slipped the pistol into the holster. Then, picking up a rifle, she checked for a full magazine, worked the action, and slid it into the passenger side rifle boot. Turning, she continued, "So where do you think they are and where do we start?"

Joe looked over at Logan and said, "I guess she's coming with."

"Rene and I had that exact conversation a few years ago. About an earlier trip into Mexico. Come on, we need to find my wife. Hopefully she's still alive."

Joe looked at the surrounding countryside. "They'll want to get across the border as soon as possible. So let's just head south and find a place we can slip across." Looking back at Logan, he said, "I know that fat guy that was with Hector is from my past. When we find them I'm going to kill him!" Slowly, he opened his shirt and said, "He gave me these. I'm going to give them back!"

Logan replied, "Let's stop in town. Hopefully we can find someone that knows this country and will tell us about the trails and canons. From there we can make some kind of a guess and hopefully find them."

Looking at Jim, Joe asked, "Hey, how well do you know this country?"

Jim replied, "I've lived here all of my life. I was born and raised just a few miles from here."

"How well do you know the desert around here? Where do you think those low life scum sucking assholes took my wife? Oh, and is there a road or trail cross country leading to Mexico?"

Jim walked over, grabbed a map and said, "Here, you can have this. I've been putting trails and seldom use roads and water holes on this for years. I've walked while hunted and searching for gold plus looking for the Lost Dutchman Mine. I've spent most of my life wandering around out there." He waved his arm across the desert horizon.

Looking at the map, Joe smiled and asked, "What can you tell us about this trail? How can we get to this trail the fastest?"

Jim looked at where Joe was pointing and said, "That trail runs along the bottom of a deep canyon with overhanging sides. Although a few days ago I was just out for a drive and I saw a camp right about here." He pointed at the map. Continuing, he said, "There were about six or seven Jeeps and probably that many tents. I just figured they were out having fun."

Joe carefully followed the road south to where he intercepted the other trails and led deeper into the desert. Looking at Jim, he asked, "It looks like there are two roads that come together here. Where does this lead to?"

Jim looked at the map, he walked over and got another. Studying the two he said, "It's an old cattle trail that leads to Mexico. There isn't an official crossing there and I can't believe anyone would take it. After you get down there, there's no water for a hundred miles or more. Plus it's so far from everything that if you have trouble no one would find you for months, maybe never."

Joe looked at Logan and smiled. "We found them. That's how they are getting across."

Looking back at Jim, he asked, "Is there anyone living down there? Somewhere we can get a few supplies?"

Jim scratched his head and said, "Yes, there's an old miners store and gas station right around here. South of there is all empty. Nothing but sand, snakes, and wet backs. It's all dry and desolate."

Joe looked around and said, "Saddle up, I think I know where they are and where they are going."

Sticking out his hand, he said, "Thanks, you've been a life saver."

Shaking hands, Logan said, "My guys should be here sometime tomorrow or the following morning. They'll get the horses out of your hair. We should be back in a week or so. Hopefully with Rene still alive. Here's the contact information for my guys and ranch. If we are not back in say two weeks call that number and have them come get the trucks and trailers." Handing Jim five one hundred dollar bills he said, "Thank you. You have know idea how much or what this means to us."

Jim handed him back the money saying, "It's too much. We can square up when you get back. I'll call your ranch if you're not back, but I won't take your money. Good hunting. I hope and pray you find her."

Joe walked over and picked up two backpacks. Looking inside, he placed one in his Wildcat and the other in Logan's. Looking at Kay, he said, "Please, honey. Please, Kay, stay here and go home with Jessie and Jerrod. I have a really bad feeling this is going to get bloody. The last time they underestimated us, this time they won't. I'm sure they know who I am and want what I'm capable of. I recognize that fat one. And when my shirt was ripped open he saw my chest. He's the asshole who put those marks there. They also know Logan's a hunter and outdoorsmen. They won't make the same stupid mistakes a second time."

Kay walked across the driveway and put her arms around him. "Honey, Joe, I know you'll protect me to the last breath. But this is a battle you can't win. I'm going to help find my friend. Next to you. Logan and Rene mean the world to me. I'll do everything in my power to help find her. So please let's get going." Reaching up, she gently kissed him then put her head against his chest as she continued to hold him tight, feeling the warmth, strength, and security in the man she loved.

She was scared and knew one or all of them could die out there in the desert. She also knew what was going through Rene's head. She had been right there just a few short years before. She has seen the brutality of Hector and his gang of human slime.

Looking at the horizon, a tear slipped from the huge cowboy as he thought about Rene. Silently he made a promise, "I'll find you, Rene, and I'll kill every fucking one of those assholes." Slowly, he turned as another tear slowly started to make its way down his cheek. Looking at Joe, he asked, "Are you ready?"

Joe looked from Logan, to Jim, then to Kay, and finally back to Logan, and said, "Let's go find her. I think we have a message to pass along. I know I do and I want to deliver it in person."

Getting into the Wildcat, he strapped in and checked Kay and then pushed the starter. Touching a couple of buttons on the GPS, he glanced at Logan and gave him a thumbs up. Logan returned the gesture and they headed out across the desert heading towards the canyon trail.

Joe's mind raced ahead as he thought about what was to come. He knew that fat prick Pablo was capable of causing unimaginable pain- Joe had been on the receiving end. Silently, he prayed that Hector would only be thinking of the money she'd bring in the human sex trade and would prevent Pablo from raping her. That was probably the kindest thing they'd do.

He knew he'd have to talk to Logan in private without Kay standing there. He had started making a plan and wanted to talk to him about it. Knowing there was still a million dollar price on his head, maybe just maybe they could make a trade. Him for her. If that happened there was a slight possibility of him escaping and making his way back.

Stopping at the top of a small rise, picked up his binoculars and scanned the desert ahead for the tell-tale sign of movement. Vehicles always caused a dust cloud that rose and drifted with the wind. It started small and spread as the car grew larger and larger. Putting down the binoculars, he continued to head for the canyon trail. Hoping that they were taking the desert road and maybe they could come out ahead of them and set up an ambush.

When they approached the canyon where the trail dropped away they stopped. Again, Joe scanned the desert ahead and behind. Seeing a small dust cloud, he continued to watch. He prayed that he'd see a flash of light off a windshield or window glass. He had noticed that the Jeeps were painted a flat color including the bumpers. That flat paint would not reflect light, although the windows still would.

Logan moved up beside him and shut the engine off. Picking up his binoculars, he saw what Joe had been watching. They sat there several minutes as he watched the dust cloud moving across the desert several miles away. Slowly, Logan puts his binoculars down and turned to look at Joe. He had seen the same thing. A flash of light off of something.

Logan asked, "Did you…?"

Joe replied, "Yeah, I did."

Logan asked, "Is it…?"

Joe put down his binoculars and looked at him. He admitted, "I don't know?"

Logan looked again and asked, "What should we do?"

"Try and get ahead of them and find out," Joe said as he hit the starter and continued, "come on, let's go."

Dropping off the plateau, they headed down the steep trail towards the canyon floor. The trail down was steep and narrow, with cliffs that dropped steeply away. One wrong turn and it was several hundred feet straight down to a certain death.

Reaching the bottom of the canyon, they found that the trail ahead was just a little less than the width of the canyon floor. It twisted and turned along with ups and downs as it followed the canyon walls. With every rise Joe would slow down and check the trail ahead while Kay continuously watched for movement or any kind of sign they were being watched.

Joe, Kay, and Logan reached the junction. Looking around, Joe walked out into the road and said, "They haven't been here yet. All these tracks are old and worn."

After hiding the two Wildcats behind a small hill with several escape routes, Joe reached into his backpack and grabbed three two-way radios. Pausing, he looked at the fourth for a minute before handing one to

Logan and another to Kay. Setting the channels, he said, "There's no cell service out here. Let's set up a crossfire ambush and wait for a couple of hours. I'm sure we are ahead of what we saw back there. If we don't see anything we'll continue south and keep searching. We have to have a place to start. This is as good as it's going to get. If it's them, let's just get her back as fast as we can and run for it."

Looking at Kay he said, "You go over by the Wildcats and wait. If I tell you to leave you head for Jim's ranch as fast as you can. There is absolutely no way those Jeeps can get through that canyon as fast as you can in one of those. Tell him what happened and stay there. When Jessie and Jerrod get here, go home." Pausing, he looked at Logan then Kay. As Kay started to speak, Joe cut her off by saying, "Damn it Kay, I mean it. If something bad happens and I'm still alive I'll find you. I've survived worse."

Logan grabbed a rifle, several clips, and a bandolier of ammo. Looking at Joe, he said, "We did this once. We can do it again." He grabbed Joe in a hug with tear filled eyes. He continued, "Thanks, buddy." Turning, he walked across the road, heading for a rock outcropping that offered great cover and a wide shooting area.

Taking Kay by the hand, they walked to where Joe wanted her to stay. Taking out her rifle, he checked to make sure it was fully loaded and said, "Once the shooting starts you listen to that radio. If I say go. You go. Don't look back, just run. Get to Jim's. I mean it Kay, I can get there on foot a lot faster than either you or Logan. So you do what I say!" Kissing her, he turned and walked towards a couple of large rocks and got ready.

For nearly an hour they waited and watched when Logan said, "There's a dust cloud headed our way. I can only see the lead vehicle. It's a Jeep. Logan continued to track the oncoming vehicle when the road turned and they all came into view. He called across the radio, "It looks like there are five- no wait, seven. Yeah, there are seven. They are all Jeeps and they're just out of the dust cloud of the next one in front. Picking up a spotting scope, he looked and said, "There are four in the front one. One of the people in the back seat has long hair. I'm sure it's Rene. Yes, now I can see Hector in the front. Get ready, it's them."

The convoy came around the last turn and Joe slowly squeezed the trigger. The front tire blew and the Jeep swerved off the road. Logan opened up on the next as guys pile out looking for cover. Joe continued to place the red dot on target after target. Hitting close enough to keep them pinned down. He glanced over at Logan who had started working his way from rock to rock towards the Jeep that he believed contained Rene. Jerking open the door, he nearly jerked her out of the seat. Logan looked into the terrified eyes of the woman he loved. Grabbing the hand cuff and the door handle, he pulled the handle loose and handed her a pistol and said run.

Logan pushed her ahead of him as he continued to shoot. Without aiming, he pulled the trigger with the barrel pointed in the direction of the slime balls he wanted to kill. Joe stepped out from behind the rocks and poured cover fire at anything that moved. Changing his fourth thirty round clip, he saw Pablo. Joe placed the red dot on his forehead as the first bullet hit him in the right arm. Looking to his right, he spun and fired, watching as the man grabbed his chest and dropped. Looking back, he again placed the red dot on Pablo's forehead. Slowly, he started to pull the trigger and was hit again, this time in the upper thigh. Joe reacquired Pablo just as he was hit for the fourth time and dropped to his knees out of sight. Picking up his radio, he called out, "Kay, run! Get the hell out of here. I'm with Logan and we'll catch you." He knew Logan couldn't hear him and knew he was hurt badly. All he wanted at this time was to know Kay was safe.

Kay jumped up and ran to the Wildcat. She hit the starter and smashed the gas to the floor as she raced back down into the canyon, this time heading north. As Logan and Rene reached the small hill they saw the retreating ATV dropping from sight. Looking around, he yelled, "Get in and hang in! Joe and Kay just left! I'm sure we can catch them!"

Joe crawled into a small area in some rocks and started looking at his wounds. He had a total of seven bullet holes. Four had gone through, although he had one low in his chest and two in his left leg where the bullet was still inside. Looking around, he saw his backpack. Getting out his first aid kit he started fixing up his wounds. He had done this before and knew how much pain he was in for.

First he poured hydrogen peroxide on the wounds that had gone clear through on his arm and leg. Then he got out a syringe of powdered quick clot. Placing it into the hole, he pushed the plunger and gritted his teeth as the powder flew into the wound. Now halfway done, he closed his eyes for a minute and started on his leg. Then he grabbed another syringe and removed the cap. It was a medical superglue. Taking a deep breath, he pushed the needle as far as he could and then pushed the plunger as he pulled out the needle. Next he placed gauze over the wounds and quickly wrapped them up.

Looking at the last two he could feel the bullet just under the top of his thigh. Using his knife he cut it open and could see the bullet. Reaching back in the first aid kit he grabbed a leatherman tool. Using the needle-nose pliers he took several deep breaths and reached inside his leg and removed the bullet. The blood slowly ran from the wound. Joe let out a breath. Slow bleeding meant no serious damage. Next he repeated the process with the quick-clot and super glue.

He removed his shirt and looked at his chest. As he breathed he saw bubbles in the blood slowly seeping from the bullet hole. Joe knew he was in serious trouble. Bubbles meant it hit a lung and the spurts meant arterial damage. Hopefully he could patch this up for now, although he knew the odds were not in his favor and he would need to have the bullet removed soon.

Laying back, he thought, *It's got to be about forty miles to Jim Steven's ranch. In the shape that I'm in, it's probably three or maybe four days walking. When Kay and Logan see I'm not with either I'm sure they come back looking for me.* While laying in his hiding spot and thinking about the walk back, he slowly drifted off.

Hector stepped on the bullet wound in Joe's leg. The pain shoots through him as he jerks wide fully awake. Looking up, he saw Hector, Juan, and Pablo looking down at him. Juan reached down and grabbed the bloody spot on his arm and jerked him to his feet, knocking him back to the rock-filled desert floor. Again he started pushing himself back up, only to be assisted by Juan who grabbed a handful of his hair and lifted him to his feet. Pushing him again Joe stumbled a few times but remained on his feet.

As he turned to face his captives, he leaned against one of the Jeeps. Pablo stepped forward, ripping open Joe's shirt and asking, "Where did you get those scars?"

Joe replies, "I dropped a razor shaving a few years ago."

Pablo drove his fist into Joe's stomach, doubling him over and dropping him to his knees. Joe looked up, coughing a few times and spitting out a mouthful of blood. Slowly, while holding on to the Jeep, he made it to his feet. Too weak to fight or run he stood his ground in defiance and stared into the eyes of three men he had sworn to kill. He wanted to kill one for what he had done so many years ago to a man named Randy. He would kill the other for what he had done a few years ago to a beautiful lady he loved named Kay. And the other one would be killed simply because he is just too cruel and stupid to be allowed to live.

Hector squeezed Joe's arm where he had been shot and asked, "Where are your friends? Where's Kay? If you don't talk I'll simply kill you and find her anyway. With you out of the picture there'll be know one to protect her."

Joe started to cough and spit out another mouthful of blood thinking, "That bullet must have gone through my lung. That's why I'm spitting up blood?

Looking at Hector, he said, "I told her to run. I really have know idea where she is."

Juan slapped him several times and asked, "Where are they? I want Rene and I want her now. I'm not going to lose her again."

Joe looked at Juan, then Hector, and finally at Pablo. "I told Kay to run. I told her I was with Logan. So she left. I'm sure Logan thinks I'm with her so they won't stop until they are back in town. If you want them I guess you can try there. Although that guy I knifed is still alive and with about a hundred cops by now. I'm sure at least a few are not on your payroll."

Hector looked at Pablo and Juan and said, "The cops are not a problem. Let's check through that canyon to see what direction they go when they leave. Maybe we can catch up before they get to town."

Suddenly someone from back in the line of Jeeps came running up calling to Hector, "Hey, Santiago wants to talk to you right away. He says it's very important."

Hector swore as he limped back to where Santiago was parked. He asked, "What's so damn important? We have captured Joe and I want Kay. I want her now."

Santiago replied, "I got it open."

"Got what opened?" asked Hector. "What the hell are you talking about?"

"The computer. I got the computer open," confirmed Santiago. "Here, watch." A few keystrokes later he said, "I got them. It looks like they are at that little ranch."

Hector looked at the computer and said, "Now tell me- how did you do it?"

Santiago replied, "Carlos has a notebook. I was reading through it and saw a few things darker than others. His wife's name, number of years they've been married, and his dads birthday. So I tried them. I had to put them in a different order once but it worked."

Hector rubbed his jaw and said, "Great, we are headed for that ranch now. Send out a group text to all of our friends on the force. Tell them not to answer any calls to that ranch. I don't want to be fighting our own people."

Limping back to where Juan and Pablo were waiting, he said, "Come on, let's get going. I want to find Kay. Then we can take him to Columbia."

Juan jerked the door open. Grabbing Joe by his wounded arm, he shoved him into the back seat and walked around just to see Pablo climbing in the back. Looking at him, he said, "I'm riding back here with him."

Pablo defied, "No, I am. I don't want you to kill him. Not until I know for sure about his scars. I think he's the ghost of Columbia. If so, he's worth a million US dollars. So you can't kill him. At least, not yet."

Joe sat and listened as they headed down into the canyon. They had searched him twice although they didn't take his belt away or figure out that the buckle was a razor sharp fighting knife with a three inch stainless steel blade that he could and would use as soon as he got a chance.

Leaving the canyon, Hector stopped and looked at the tracks. "It looks like they are headed for that little ranch."

Looking at Juan, he said, "Call Santiago and the rest. Make sure that you are ready." Looking at Joe, he continued, "I'm quite sure they are. They'll have cover and we'll be in the open. So we need to figure this out before just trying to take them. Remember that damn cowboy is a very good shot and so are both women."

Juan called the rest saying, "We've found them! I'll send you our location. Get here as quickly as you can."

Pulling Joe by the arm and hair he said, "How many are there? What kind of guns do you have?"

Slapping him, he said, "Answer me! Answer me or I'll just kill you now and make the attack anyway."

Pablo stepped between Joe and Juan and said, "I told you we couldn't kill him. I have to find out where he got those scars. I think I gave them to him several years ago. He's the ghost of Columbia and he's worth a lot of money."

Turning, he looked at Joe and said, "Have you been to Columbia? I gave you those scars. I want an answer. Are you the ghost? The Columbians will give me a million dollars to keep you alive." Looking at Hector and then at Juan, "Did you hear that? Alive!"

Joe looked him in the eyes and whispered, "You'll never live long enough to collect a penny of that."

Pablo turned back to Joe and said, "What did you say? You are the ghost. I knew it. I gave you those scars."

Joe looked and said, "Who, me? I never said a thing."

Hector looked at Pablo and said, "'We can take him to Columbia after we get the rest. Juan wants Rene and he also wants to kill that damn cowboy. I simply want Kay. I don't care what you do with him. Although for now you need to shut up. I need to think. We need to make a plan."

With the rest of the gang arriving, Hector started to point at people and boss then in various directions, "You two go around and stay out of sight. You and you follow them and stay off to the side. You and you go on this side and stop where you can see the front and side. Juan and I will watch from here. If you see anyone other than the two women, kill them. Diego, I want you to take him over there and keep him quiet." He pointed to a huge pile of rocks.

With everything set up, Hector moved a little closer to the house and called out, "Hey! In the house! We have you completely surrounded. Send out the two women and we'll just take them and leave. If you try to fight you will all die."

Just then, the red and blue lights flashed on and all hell broke loose. Hector and his group of human waste opened fire at the house, the cops, and anything that moved. Inside the house Logan grabbed Rene and Kay, knocking them to the floor and holding them down while bullets ricocheted away or embedded themselves in the walls.

Both Officer Davis and Officer Jackson were hit in the first few seconds and lay bleeding on the floor. Jim had dropped to the floor behind the couch just as Logan knocked both Kay and Rene down. He told them to stay down and he carefully worked his way to a window. Slowly, he slid the rifle into position and squeezed the trigger several times.

Joe looked at Diego who was watching the gun fight. Joe's hand worked slowly to his belt and removed the buckle knife. Coming up from behind, Diego spun, swinging his rifle like a club. Joe kept his left hand with the knife out of sight, giving Diego the false security that Joe was hurt worse that he was. As Diego charged, Joe pivoted on one leg, driving the knife into the base of Diego's skull.

Still holding the knife in his hand, he gave it a little twist as Diego sank to the ground. Joe looked at the light and muscles flashed everywhere. Picking up Diego's M-16, Joe found several full magazines and suddenly he was back in Afghanistan.

It was a patrol of Army Rangers. They had been ambushed by an overwhelming force of Taliban. With a few carefully placed shots, he would move and set up again, always taking just a few shots and moving. Thus making it nearly impossible for someone to zero in on his location as he continued to rain fire and hell on the gang of human trafficking slime. The shots got fewer and fewer. Taking careful aim, he would take two or three shots. As he started to move he felt the burn of a bullet as it hit him in the upper leg. Knocking him off his feet and actually saving his life from a full clip that was sprayed where he had been standing just a second earlier. Carefully, he started crawling and worked his way to get within twenty feet of the back door as he saw the first of several vehicles leave. Heading straight out into the desert.

Joe got to his feet. Taking a few steps, he stumbled and fell, crawling the last couple of yards. He reached the door and worked his way back to his feet. Kay heard something or someone stumble around close to the back door. Careful not to expose herself, she looked through the window and screamed. Yanking the door open, she saw Joe standing there. Their eyes locked for a few seconds. She stared into the eyes of the man she loved. Severely wounded with blood running everywhere, Joe said, "Did you miss me?"

Then with a half-hearted smile, he took a few steps and started to fall headlong through the door. Kay ran forward, catching Joe and trying to stop him from hitting the floor. Although his weight was too much and they both hit the floor. Kay slowly rolled him to his side. Then she rolled him over into her lap and started trying to stop the flow of blood as tears continued to pour from her eyes.

CHAPTER ELEVEN

Kay sat there trying to stop the bleeding as Rene continued to bring her what she needed. Logan checked on the two officers laying on the floor as Jim watched the surrounding area for signs of movement.

With the only movement outside being the flashing lights of the sheriff's car, he went to help Logan make sure the two officers would survive.

When the gun fight started, a few calls for backup went out. Two more deputies answered the call along with emergency personnel.

The wounded were taken away by ambulance or in a squad car, depending on the severity of their injuries. Gunshot victims were taken first. Joe was loaded into one of the first ambulances and was still holding Kay's. It was a rough ride down the ten miles of dirt road to the highway.

Arriving at the hospital, Kay kissed Joe as a surgical team rushed him away. A few minutes later, a deputy walked in and started asking questions. Logan walked in and watched through the tears and sobs as Kay tried to answer the questions. The officer kept firing question after question. With tears pouring from her eyes, Kay would go from one to another giving partial answers.

Logan stepped forward between Kay and the over zealous officer and said, "That's enough questions. Her husband is the one who saved us and several of your friends and fellow officers. He's in surgery all shot to shit and not doing very well. Keep your questions and your horse shit attitude to yourself. Better yet get the hell out of here. We'll answer you after he's out and we know the outcome!"

Five hours later doctor Jayson Williams walked into the waiting room and asked for Kay West. She stood up and said, "I'm Kay," as she slowly walked towards the doctor. Turning, she looked at Logan and motioned him to follow. As one, Logan and Rene stood up and walked towards the door and followed doctor Williams towards a private room. Stopping, he opened the door for Kay but stepped in front of Logan and Rene saying, "I'm sorry, but family only."

Kay put her hand in the doctor's arm and said, "It's okay, I want them here no matter what you have to say."

Stepping back as Logan and Rene followed Kay into the conference room, the doctor closed the door and said, "He's out of surgery and in recovery. You can see him in a few minutes. He is in terrible shape. With several bullet wounds. One passed through the side of his lung. That was the worst but we did get the bleeding to stop. After that it was a total nightmare. We had to clean and close several others along with more internal damage. We have him on a strong antibiotic drip and he's still sedated. He's lost a lot of blood and as of now all you can do is pray."

Logan slowly turned Kay so she was facing him. Wrapping his arms around her, he could feel as she cried and shook in his arms. With her breath coming in deep gasps, she continued to shake as she finally asked, "When- umm- when can I see him?"

Doctor Williams reached out and touched her arm and said, "I'll let you in now. Please be as quiet as you can." Then looking at Logan and Rene, he said, "You can see him also. But please only for a few minutes."

Looking at Rene, Logan said, "We'll go in after Kay spends as much time as she wants."

Kay broke in by saying, "I won't be leaving. I don't care what you say. He's my husband and I'll sit at his side and hold his hand. I'll do whatever you say except leave. So you had better just accept that now."

Looking at Logan, she said, "Come on, let's go see him."

Opening the door, Kay slowly walked to Joe's side. Picking up his hand, she placed it against her cheek. Bending forward, she kissed his forehead and lips. Then putting one hand on top and the other below, she slowly sunk down into the chair that Logan had moved to Joe's bedside.

After spending just a few minutes Logan couldn't take it anymore. Reaching over Kay, he said, "I'll be just outside the door. I won't let anyone into this room unless they absolutely have to be here. Rubbing Joe's shoulder, he took Rene's hand and slowly walked out of the room. Looking at Rene, he said, "Wait here. I'll be back in a few minutes."

Leaving the hospital, he walked to his pickup and got his .44 magnum. Finding his shoulder holster and strapping it on, he grabbed 6 quick loaders for his hand cannon. Checking to make sure it was loaded he slipped it into the holster and put on a light jacket. Looking through the parking lot, he headed back inside.

Walking down the hall, Logan saw a law enforcement officer. Stopping, he sat down next to him and asked, "Are you going to post an officer outside Joe's room?"

The officer asked, "Why would we need to do that?"

Logan replied, "Well, let's see. Kay was kidnapped by Hector a year ago. Then they came all the way to Montana to try again. My wife was taken after the free for all in town a few days ago and now they nearly killed him in an attempt to get the two women again. A few years ago we learned that Hector has been wanted on both sides of the border. There are two DEA agents about a hundred miles south of here. They have been trying to catch him. Now we find out he's been operating through this area and you guys can't catch him."

Officer Steve Bishop walked up to Logan, stuck out his chest and asked, "What are you trying to say?"

Logan stood up and turned, looking down at the sheriff's deputy. He said, "I'm not saying anything. Only that's it's funny that a drug running human trafficking slime ball like Hector and Juan travel through this area and you guys didn't know or maybe you didn't care. Like maybe he's paying you or someone to look the other way. Now I'm asking if you are going to post a guard and watch Joe's room? Or do I have to do your job here and watch both women as well?"

Deputy Steve said, "Let me check and see. Although I really doubt we will post anyone here. The attack was your fault."

Logan grabbed him by the shirt, jerking him forward and lifting him off his feet. He slammed him up against the wall and said, "They took Kay once, then they tried a second time. Next they took Rene and nearly killed Joe. Maybe you don't care but I do. So either you post someone here or I'll stand guard. Either way, someone is going to watch and if you do it then I'll be watching you. So just be warned that if anything happens here I'll be close enough to find out and whoever is at fault will pay!"

Letting him go, Logan turned to walk away when officer Bishop said, "I'm a law enforcement officer and you just assaulted me. I could arrest you for that."

Logan stopped. He looked at him and said, "Assault you? Buddy, if I assaulted you, you would know it. You would be laying on the ground bleeding severely and unconscious. So remember that and do your damn job."

Walking down the hall, Logan grabbed a chair and placed it next to the door. Opening the door slowly, he saw Kay next to Joe's bed. Still holding his hand and slowly stroking his hair. Kay turned her head and looked at Logan. She smiled weakly with tears still pouring from eyes. She looked back at her husband. Looking around, he saw Rene sitting in a chair just a few feet away. Closing the door, he took up his post and sat back. No one, absolutely no one, would get in that room that was not supposed to be there. Reaching inside his jacket, he checked to make sure his hand cannon is secure but not strapped in.

As day became night Logan asked for two recliners. He carried the first into Joe's room, telling Kay to get up as he placed it next to Joe's bed. A few minutes later, he carried another in and placed it a few feet away.

"Why don't you try and get some sleep?" said Rene. "I'll watch outside and wake you if anything happens or doesn't look right."

Logan was dead tired after being up nearly twenty-four hours and said, "That sounds like a great idea. Do you have your pistol?"

Rene opened her coat and said, "Between you and Joe I don't go anywhere anymore without this." Letting her coat close, she opened the door and sat down to let Logan get a couple hours of much needed sleep. Sitting there, she watched as nurses and doctors made their way up and down the halls. She saw someone walk around the corner, stop, turn around, and disappear. Getting up, she walked down the hall and peaked around the corner only to see them disappear into an elevator. Watching the elevator, she saw it stop on the floor above. Walking back to the stairway, she carefully opened the door and heard footsteps coming down towards her. Closing the door, she stepped back and waited.

As the door opened Rene removed her Glock 19 from its holster and pressed it against her leg. Two Hispanics walked down the hall towards Joe's room. Stopping, one drew a bottle with a rag hanging from the end just as Rene brought the pistol up and said, "If you both want to die just try and light that."

Both guys snapped around and looked down the barrel of her 9MM as the door flew open behind them. They turned to look at the wild eyes of a pissed off cowboy. Logan reached out and took the firebomb in his left hand. Drawing back, he let his right go. Connecting solid with one of them, Rene brought down the barrel of her pistol on the back of the other's skull. With two guys laying on the floor, a doctor ran down the hall and asked, "What's going on here and why did you do this to these two guys?"

Logan handed him the firebomb as Rene said, "They were about to light that and throw it into Joe's room. Logan must have heard me yell and came out while I was trying to figure out what to do next. Joe needs police protection."

Doctor Calvin Hanna said, "Yes, he does. Although I don't think he'll get it from our local law enforcement. You didn't hear this from me but I don't trust any of them. I'm really surprised any of you are still alive. I can't prove it although it's clear to many of us. They are all on Hector's payroll."

Logan stepped out of the room and walked to stand next to Rene as the doctor turned to walk away. Picking up his phone, he calls the sheriff's department. When they answered, Logan said, "This is Logan. I'm at the hospital. I need a cruiser here as soon as possible. There are two guys laying on the floor bleeding. If they wake up before you get here then we'll also need the coroner. They tried to firebomb a room here."

Ten minutes later Officers Jose Lois and Miguel Angel walked up and asked, "What did you do now?"

Logan replied, "Caught two of your friends trying to firebomb a room."

Jose stuck out his chest and said, "What do you mean our friends? What are you saying? Maybe we should arrest you for assault?"

Logan stepped forward and said, "Just try that and you two will be laying next to them. So just pick their sorry worthless asses up and take them to jail. I'll be down to file charges later along with people from the hospital and they had better be there- or else."

Miguel stepped forward and said, "Or else what?"

Logan smiles. "You'll find out. And I'm quite sure you won't like it."

Logan and Rene watched as the two Officers helped the other two to their feet. Handcuffing them, they lead them down the hall towards the elevator. Looking at Rene, he said, "I'm awake now, why don't you try and sleep. I'm sure it's going to be a couple of very long days before Joe is ready to leave here and we get somewhere safe."

Rene said, "Oh hey, I almost forgot. Jessie and Jerrod are here. They got the horses and are going to stop and see Joe before they head for home.

Looking at his watch, Logan said, "Wow, they made great time. They must have driven nearly straight through."

Opening the door, Rene walked back inside and rubbed Joe's shoulder, giving Kay a quick hug before tucking the Glock between her leg and the side of the chair. Reclining back, she closed her eyes to get a quick nap before relieving Logan in a few hours.

As Logan sat down, his ranch foreman and number one hand walked around the corner. Logan quickly stood up and walked to meet them.

"It's great to see you guys. Joe is in there so please be very quiet. He's all shot to shit and in terrible shape. The doctors said all we can do is pray. He is tough but he's lost a lot of blood. Oh, and Kay is a mess so please make your visit short."

Jessie opened the door and slowly stepped inside. Kay stood up and wrapped her arms around the ranch foreman and said, "My god, it's good to see you." Stepping back, she let him walk over and sit down next to Joe.

With tears starting to run down his cheeks, he put his hand on Joe's shoulder and said, "Come on buddy, fight. You're stronger than this." Looking at Kay, he slowly got up. He walked over and wrapped his arms around her again, whispering, "We all love him too. He's stronger than any of us know. I know he'll be okay. He has to be. He promised to help me get a mountain goat next year. I drew a tag for the area around the ranch." Smiling, he kissed Kay on the cheek and continued, "Jerrod is outside the door with Logan. He wants to see him also." Walking over, he hugged Rene then turned and walked out the door.

A few minutes later, the door opened again as Jerrod walked in followed by Logan and Jessie. Rene got up and walked to the door. Holding it open, she could see what was going on both in the hall and in the room. As all three men stood there looking down at Joe, Kay walked in between them and said, "I know he'll be alright. It's just so hard to see him lying here like this. He's always on the go doing something."

While everyone was standing there, Rene walked in looking at Joe. She slid her hand into Logan's and gave him a squeeze. They talked about what happened when Kay said, "I think there's a pizza place in town. Let's order a pizza before the guys leave. I haven't eaten anything since yesterday and I'm starved."

Looking from Logan to Rene, then at Jessie and Jerrod, she asked, "Oh, come on, are any of you hungry? I can't be the only one."

Forty-five minutes later all four were sitting around a small table that Logan had found and carried to just outside Joe's room. With several pizzas arriving, they invited anyone that walked by to have a piece. An hour later Jessie and Jerrod stood up and started saying goodbye to everyone. Walking in the room, they both touched Joe's shoulder. With everything ready, they headed for Montana and the Rocking L. Kay and Rene walked back into the room. Kay went straight to where her husband was still lying unconscious. Bending forward, she kissed his forehead and sat down next to him. Picking up his hand, she watched as Joe fought for his life. Rene quietly walked to her chair. Placing her pistol between her leg and the chair, she silently cried as she watched Kay.

Logan sat down outside the room. Checking his hand cannon, he leaned back against the wall and started thinking about all the great times he had with Joe. Looking down the hall, he watched as a huge black man and a smaller white guy came walking down the hall. Standing up, Logan's hand instinctively went inside his coat and wrapped around the grip of his pistol. With his thumb on the hammer and his finger already on the trigger, he watched as they walked closer and closer.

The Black man put both of his hands up and said, "Woah, slow down cowboy. If who I think is in that room is in that room, then I've known more about him and have known him longer than you."

Logan looked at the huge man, all six-foot eight inches and two hundred and seventy pounds of him. Something seemed and looked familiar. Stepping closer and still holding onto his pistol, he said, "Before you come any closer. You had better tell me who you are and how you know him. Or you are probably not going to like the outcome!"

With both hands still open and palms facing up he said, "Can I please get closer? What I have to say is very private and I don't want anyone to overhear us."

Removing the pistol from the holster and holding it straight down with the hammer back and his finger still on trigger, Logan motioned him forward. Then just out of reach he said, "Okay, that's close enough."

The huge man looked around and said, "I knew him when his name was Randal Jackson. I'm Adrian Sawyer."

Logan smiled. "You were at their wedding in Colorado."

Adrian smiled too. "Try Illinois. Just west of Chicago. In that little country church. Now may I ask who you are and if the guy in there is named Joe West?"

Logan released the trigger, letting the hammer slowly fall back to the safe position and slipping his trusty hand cannon back into its holster. Sticking out his hand, he said, "I'm Logan Lathrop."

Shaking hands, Adrian motioned for Colton Savage to join them and said, "They served together in Afghanistan. I was his captain and handler while he was in Columbia."

Shaking hands, Colton said, "I was his Sargent while he was in training. I helped hone his natural abilities. He is by far the best I have ever seen. After his time in the Middle East we got together several times and stayed in touch after that. I was at his wedding and met you there."

Logan stepped back a couple of steps and said, "Yes, yes I remember you now. Anyway, yes, he's in that room. We, umm, he has had some trouble with a couple of Mexicans. It seems they want Kay and now Rene. I'm sorry to say but neither Joe or I are willing to give the girls up without a fight. A couple years ago they took Kay. Joe called me and I left for Mexico that afternoon. Last year they came to Montana and tried again."

Logan opened the door and slowly walked in followed by Adrain and Colton. Rene sprang to her feet, pistol up and pointed at the two men following her husband. Logan's hands went up as he said, "It's okay-calm down. They both know Joe."

As Rene lowered her pistol, Kay jumped to her feet and ran to the huge man. Wrapping her arms around him, she asked, "How on earth did you find us?"

Adrian looks at Logan then Rene and back to Kay as she assured him, "It's okay, you can talk in front of them. I know a lot about Joe's past and Logan and Rene both know some." Turning, she looked at her husband and said, "He's the only reason I'm still alive and a big part of why they are."

Adrian looked at each of them in turn, then at Colton. Colton stepped forward and said, "So much of what he has done is still classified that we could actually end up in prison if anyone ever found out we told you. So all I'm going to say is that we have been keeping tabs on him. We have been ever since the run in at the mountain retreat he was building."

Kay's mouth dropped open as she said, "How did you know about that?"

Adrian replied, "Joe contacted the department I worked for. Someone there found a note about the call and contacted me. We sent people to his cabin and did a search of the area. They found two people lying at the bottom of a cliff. It was ruled an accident by the local authorities. Although we also found the tell tale signs of a very short but violet fight in his driveway. That told us everything we needed to know. When everything was put together I started looking for him. I contacted Colton and together we have been searching the web looking for news releases like the one we found here in Arizona. Colton found the release and contacted me. We went over the story and made a few phone calls. Next thing I know I'm standing in front of Logan here looking at the wrong end of a very large gun held by a man I knew without a doubt could use it."

Adrian looked around for a second. Then looking at Colton, he said, "Let's go get a couple of rooms. We need to stay until Joe wakes up. We really need to talk with him." Pausing, he walked to Kay and said, "We will be back in an hour or so. Here's my card. If he wakes up before that please call me."

Then looking at Logan, he said, "We will help you stand guard, you look just a little tired and jumpy. I would hate to surprise you. I'm thinking you're very capable of hitting something with that cannon under your jacket."

Adrian and Colton walked out the door and headed for the only motel in town. Adrian opened the door and walked up to the desk. Showing his government ID, he said, "We need two rooms for about a week. It may be longer with a slight possibility of being shorter."

The man behind the counter replied, "I'm sorry, but I don't believe we have any rooms available."

Colton stepped forward and produced his Military Special Forces ID and said, "Maybe you had better look again or my next call will be the pentagon, and I'm quite sure they could contact someone you don't want to deal with, so get us two rooms before I reach across the counter and simply snap your neck."

The man looked at the door just as a sheriff's deputy walked in and repeated, "Sir, we don't have any rooms. So I advise you to call whoever you want before that man behind you simply throws both of your asses in jail."

Colton turned around and for a few seconds he stared at the deputy before a large smile crossed his face. His longtime friend and corporal Chance Reed was standing just a few feet away. In the matter of a few seconds the two men recognized each other and they both stepped forward, grasping hands and ending up in a huge hug.

Colton, still laughing and smiling, said, "Chance, this is special agent Adrian Sawyer. Adrian this is Chance Reed. We served together for several years. He is one of the best trainers we have. He helped train you-know-who."

Chance looked at the two men and asked, "Are you guys staying long?"

Colton replied, "We are trying to get a room although this nice gentleman behind the counter says that they are full."

Chance looked at the guy and said, "Hey Jimmy, is that right? Are you full?"

Jimmy looked at Chance and said, "It sure looks that way. Although let me check again." Pausing he said, "Let me make a couple of phone calls and confirm these reservations. Just to make sure."

Chance replied, "Here's my card. Call me as soon as you know. We'll be cross the street having a cold one." Looking at Colton, he continued. "I'm off-duty so I'll change my shirt in the car. I'll catch up with you two in a few minutes."

Colton shook his friend's hand again and said, "That sounds great. See you in a few." He pushed Adrian ahead of him and together they walked across the street.

Once out of the building, he looked at Adrian and said, "There's something going on in this town that I don't like. Keep your eyes open and make sure you can get inside your jacket at all times. I'm not sure but I think maybe the whole town is protecting that drug-running prick."

A few minutes later Chance walked in. Looking around carefully, he slowly sat down and whispered, "You two keep your eyes open at all times. You are not safe here; most of this town relies on the money Hector pays to keep his activities quiet. I've been here for about six months and it's not good. I've been collecting intel for the DEA and

I'm about done. I'm sure they'll come in and there's going to be a huge bust. Although from what I have found out so far they'll fight and they are heavily armed. Fully automatic weapons. Hector has a lot of people on his payroll. Like that low life asshole Jimmy. Oh and by the way there are a couple of rooms although I think it would be better for you to drive about thirty miles south and stay there. Like I said, Hector owns this town and most of the sheriff's department with it. Everything I've have found out so far there are only a handful of guys not on his payroll and they just keep their mouths shut and leave as soon as they can find another job. This county is so corrupt even the judge is paid."

Adrain slowly stood up and said, "Let's walk, I want to be somewhere, where no one can hear us." Dropping a ten dollar bill on the table the four men walked out into the bright afternoon Arizona sun. Turning left, they walked towards the outskirts of town when Adrain stopped and looked around. Seeming to make a decision, he said, "Chance, do you remember Randy Jackson?"

Chance smiled and said, "How could I not remember him? He is by far the best man to ever come out of our training program at Fort Bragg." Then looking at Colton, he asked, "Are they still doing that program?"

Colton replied, "Absolutely, but they'll never find another Randy. He has more confirmed kills than anyone either before or after- along with what he did in Columbia after. He is nothing short of a living legend."

Chance replied, "Yes, I heard about Columbia and his action there. The people I work with still talk about him."

Adrian looked at Colton, then Chance, and said, "He's in the hospital here. Seems like someone wants him dead."

Chance looked from Adrain to Colton and said, "Really, Randy Jackson is here." Pausing, he looked into the clear blue Arizona sky and continued, "Did he have something to do with that fight in town a few days ago? I was off that day and drove to Tucson to make a report. Anyway, when I got back here everyone was still talking about it. It seems like he didn't step on someone's toes- but he stomped on them and half the department was still screaming about it."

Colton looked at Adrian and nodded as Adrian said, "It seems like someone on the inside leaked information about him to some people in Columbia, although they didn't know his name, they simply said he is still alive. Now what we have found out so far is that the Colombian Cartels have put yet another contract out on him. But so far they haven't been able to locate him to try anything, that all ended a few days ago. Seems like the guy that tortured him in Columbia several years ago thought he may have recognized him. We have an informant with that gang. He let us know so we could get to him first. I don't think we had better let him know. I'm quite sure he'll go looking for them and right now that wouldn't be a good deal. I think we had just better stay close and if something happens then tell him."

Chance looked from Colton to Adrian and said, "I'll keep my eyes and ears open and report anything I hear to you. If it comes to a fight, I'll get to you hopefully before it starts. That way you'll have one more law enforcement officer on your side. Oh, I can also bring some fire power and ammunition."

Colton said, "I think we are going to stay at that fleabag hotel in town. I'm sure we can set up some kind of security to protect us while sleeping. Besides, I really want to stay close to him during all this. Thirty miles is just too far if trouble starts."

Chance replied, "Maybe I should just pull the plug here and join forces with you. If I tell Tucson about Randy being here they'll order me to. I think the entire department would show up to help him."

Adrain looked around and said, "No, we need you on the inside if you hear or see anything." Pausing, he watched as a couple of guys started walking in their direction. As his hand slowly slid inside his coat, he glanced at Chance and he said, "Hey, do you know those two?"

Chance looked down the street and said, "Yes, Angel and Jorge Martin. Two trouble causers. It's rumored they work for Hector, although no one has ever been able to prove it. A couple of months ago two dead bodies were found in the desert north of here, both were male. We identified them and notified their families. They asked about the two girls with them. We never did find the girls." Pausing he walked towards the two guys just to have them change direction and walk away. Coming back he said, "I know they had something to do with it although I still can't prove it."

Colton glanced at Chance and said, "Looks like they don't want to talk to us?"

Chance replied, "Not unless they catch us alone or if there were three or four more with them. Watch your backs. They'll back shoot you or jump you from behind depending on what their orders are and right now, I'm sure they still want someone alive. Come on, let's go see how he is doing. Besides, I want to meet him."

Arriving at the hospital, they walked around a corner only to have Logan stand up with his hand cannon already out and the hammer back. Chance stops suddenly, backs up a few steps and putting his hands up he says , "Whoa, cowboy."

Adrian stepped around and said, "He's with us. He's a good guy. He served with Randy- I mean Joe." Pausing, he looked at Chance and said, "His name is Joe, Joe West. From now on that's the only name we use." As the door opened, Rene came up in a two handed stance with her pistol aimed.

Logan looked at her as Rene quickly took a step to the side. Glancing at Kay, she saw she was also standing with her pistol trained on the newcomer behind Logan just as Adrian filled the door. With the tense moment over, both Kay and Rene slowly lowered their guns as Adrain made introductions. Kay smiled and laid her pistol on the bed next to Joe as Rene took a few more steps to the side, keeping her gun in her hand.

Chance said, "Here, let me remove the tension here." Slowly, he reached for his side arm with just his thumb and forefinger. Slowly and carefully, he lifted it from the holster and handed it to Colton. Looking at Kay, then Rene, he smiled and said, "Is that better ladies? I am on your side."

Kay smiled and replied, "We are all a little jumpy with all that has happened." Looking at her husband, she wiped the tears from her eyes again and said, "We are just trying to save him now. After what he did to save all of us."

Chance stepped forward, putting his hand on Joe's shoulder. He said, "I knew who he was in the service and again while he was in Columbia. Although I never dreamt I would meet him again. From what I was told he never left Columbia,"

Rene said, "I sure wish everyone thought that. It would make what we have planned so much easier." Looking at Kay, then Logan, she sighed and said, "As soon as Joe wakes up with the doctor's help we are going to take him out of here and run for that place he has way out in the desert. We talked with our favorite rancher and he's getting everything ready so it'll be fast and easy. One minute we are here and the next, gone. No one will know where we went or when we left. We have already made the calls and talked with everyone. I think the doctor wants him gone as badly as we want to leave."

Logan looked at Adrian and said, "Any chance you guys want to stand watch tonight. We could all really use a good night's sleep."

Adrain looked at Colton, then Chance, and asked, "You two came to help out. I know I'm going to." Glancing at Logan, he said, "Yes, I'll sit in the haul."

Colton replied, "I'll stand guard in here."

Chance reached for his police radio and said, "Here, take this. I have a few more in the car. I'll keep one and watch from the parking lot." Changing the radio channel, he continued, "I had four radios specialized in Tucson by the DEA. They have an extra channel that only the DEA uses around here. They won't reach the border but they'll work great for us tonight. If I see anything, I can warn you two to get ready."

With everyone looking at Chance, Kay glanced back at Joe just in time to see him trying to get out of bed. With a muffled cry, she grabbed Joe's arm just seconds ahead of Logan, who picked him up and said, "You damn idiot. How long have you been awake? What the hell are you thinking? You've been unconscious for over a week."

Joe shook his head and said, "A week. What the hell happened? Logan, put me down." Shaking his head again, he saw Kay. Smiling he said, "If I've been out for a week. We have some catching up to do." Slowly, Logan put him down. Letting him go, Joe took a couple of steps sideways.

Kay made a grab for him and said, "You had better sit down before you fall down."

Smiling, Joe replied, "Just give me a minute. Let me get my shit together. Damn, why do I hurt everywhere?" Pausing, he looked at his legs, then chest, and said, "What happened and where are we?"

Slowly, Kay helped lower him back into bed and said, "We had a gun fight with Hector's gang. You got shot several times. You made it to the ranch house and fell through the back door. I thought you were dead. The doctors here said you had about a fifty-fifty chance of surviving the surgery and probably less after. We have been standing guard. They tried once more to kill you or maybe us. As soon as possible we are getting out of here and the hell out of this area."

Joe slowly laid back down as Kay covered him up. Joe looked into the loving eyes of his wife and said, "No, we have a vacation planned and I have unfinished business with Hector and that fat prick."

As she continued to watch, Joe closed his eyes and drifted off.

Sitting down, she glanced at everyone else and said, "I know my husband and that tone. We are leaving either tomorrow or the next day. Although we won't be going very far."

Early the following morning, Joe's eyes started to flutter as he slowly woke up. Carefully, he sat up and looked around the room. Something wasn't right although he has no idea what. Seeing Kay sleeping in a chair next to him, he instantly started to smile until he noticed the pistol in her hand. Tears slowly started trickling down his face as he thought, *Okay, Randy now look at the mess you're in. How could you have thought it would be possible for you to live a normal life? Now the Columbians know you're still alive. How in the hell are you going to protect her?* Pausing, he saw Rene also sleeping with a pistol in her hand. Pushing himself to an upright position -carefully and quietly as the trained warrior he was- Joe slipped out of bed. With all of his senses on high alert, he made his way to the bathroom. Slowly he pulled the door open. Just as a man yelled and jumped at him. Joe's training instantly came to the surfaces. His left fist came up in a bone-crushing strike to the man's throat. Followed by a right fist that sunk into his solar plexus, connecting just a shade high. The man grabbed for his throat as he doubled over and dropped to the floor.

Joe spun as he heard the door crashing open and bouncing off the wall. Logan followed by Adrain, Colton, and Chance came crashing into the room. Kay and Rene were instantly on their feet with both of them pointing their guns at the window. Kay screamed as she saw Joe leaning against the wall and slipping towards the floor. In a couple of steps, she had her arms around him, trying to keep him from sliding farther down. Just as she gets him stopped. Adrian's huge arms slipped in and lifted him back to a standing position.

Joe's eyes came back into focus as he started to recognize everyone except Chance, who was kneeling by the man on the floor. Looking up, he said, "No need to worry about this guy. He's dead."

Joe looked over his shoulder. Shaking his head trying to clear his thoughts, he stuttered, "I- umm- I- I didn't hit him that hard."

Chance replied, "Maybe not but his throat was crushed and I'm sure he has a couple of broken ribs. There's one that's broken twice and it's out of place. From what I can tell it's pushed in and up. I'm sure it's either in a lung or possibly his heart."

Pausing, Joe took a deep breath. Looking around, he finally said, "Logan, Rene, you need to know something so you can decide if you want to stay or head for home." Taking a second deep breath, he said, "It's me they want and I'm sure they won't stop." As he placed his hand against the wall and took a couple of shaky steps in the thief's direction.

Adrian stepped in and said, "His real name is Randy Jackson. He's probably the best special ops sniper that the military ever trained. Now he's retired from the military and DEA. He spent nearly four years in the Middle East doing what he's trained to do. That is simply to kill terrorists. After that the DEA got a hold of him, he spent ten years as a deep cover operative in Columbia. Where he continued to do what he's trained to do. To put it in simple terms: search and destroy."

As Adrian took a breath, Chance said, "I heard about him in both the military and DEA. He's a living legend in both branches."

As Chance pauseed, Colton spoke up saying, "I helped with his training. There is no doubt about his training. He's probably one of the best trained, most skilled operators to ever come out of Ft. Bragg. Nonone there could believe what they were seeing. They threw everything they could think of at him and he just kept coming out on top. We started calling him the ghost. He would pop up, causing more trouble than any single guy could possibly cause. They simply melted back into the forest. We even tried tracking him with dogs. No good, they couldn't stay on his trail. In the Middle East his reputation arrived ahead of him. After a couple of months the Taliban stayed in their camps at night. Some said they actually started believing he was a ghost. His call sign stayed with him all the way to Columbia. From what other agents have told us, the cartels hated him and tried more than once to capture him, setting up ambushes all over the country to no avail. He would spot the trap and either avoid it or cause so much trouble they finally gave up. They never even got close."

Adrian looked around and said, "Most everything we've told you is somewhat classified. As of now he's in the witness protection program. His cover has already been blown once. I don't need to tell you what happened. Now it looks like that fat friend of Hectors may have recognized him. This is going to be troublesome if what we think is true, is true. The Colombian Cartels will stop at nothing to capture or kill him. So you need to make a decision. I think it would be wise if you went home and took Kay with you. I know Joe won't run. We also know that Hector wants Kay. Now, this it's not your fight. The best way to keep her safe is to get her as far away as possible from Hector and his plans."

Pausing, he looked from Kay to Logan at the back, and continued, "She has to be somewhere safe and protected. That means as far away from here as possible."

Kay spun on her heel and said, "I'm not going anywhere! That man is my husband." As she pointed at Joe who was now leaning against the wall. "He's saved my life so many times. If he's going, I'm going. I would rather die at his side than to live one day without him. So you can forget that. I love him more than life."

Logan smiled as he replied, "I'm staying." Looking at Rene, he asked, "Honey?"

Rene stepped forward, still holding her pistol. Looking from Kay to Joe, she replied, "It's not even a question. I'm staying. I'll die fighting to protect my husband." As she walked to Logan she continued, "After what Joe did a few days ago. Well, there's absolutely no way I could leave. I'm staying!"

The next three days passed with no trouble. On the morning of the fourth day, Joe's doctor walked in. After a very thorough examination, he said, "I believe you're strong enough to leave the hospital as long as you follow all orders," after a short conversation between the doctor and Joe.

Kay reached over and put her hand over his mouth, she said, "Doctor. If he doesn't do what I tell him he'll be back with at least one broken leg."

Doctor Dias smiled slightly as he turned away from Joe. Looking at Kay, he replied, "We have been fighting with him for three days about doing what he needs to do." Pausing, he looked around and then back to Kay and said, "I think I would pay to see that. In fact I'll set his leg free." Turning back to Joe, he said, "I'll sign your release as long as you do what she says. Oh, and by the way, if she breaks your leg I'll be playing golf for at least a couple of more hours while you sit in pain."

Shaking Joe's hand and then everyone else's, he said, "I'll be back with his discharge orders which I'll hand to you," as he shook Kay's hand he continued, "in just a few minutes."

PART TWO

BLOOD IN THE DESERT SAND

Twenty minutes later Doctor Pedro Dias walked back into the room with Joe's release paperwork and a wheelchair. Handing the paperwork to Joe, he said, "Here. Would you please sign these?"

"Should I read them first?" Joe asked.

"Sure," Doctor Dias shrugged. "I have an hour to kill. I'll just stand over there and talk to that pretty wife of yours."

Joe chuckled. "Ha, ha. She doesn't need any encouragement." Grabbing a pen, he quickly signed the discharge paperwork.

Doctor Dias walked over and started to help Joe to stand up. He said, "Here, have a seat and I'll wheel you out."

"I can walk," Joe replied. "I've been walking since before I was two."

Doctor Dias replied, "Sorry, hospital rules. You have to be wheeled out."

Joe looked at the wheelchair and then the doctor and said, "Looks like there's been a change in the rules. I'm walking!"

Kay quickly stepped forward. "Joe, honey, you were shot several times. You lost a lot of blood. You spent nearly six hours in surgery. No matter what you may think, you are still not as strong as you think you are. I nearly lost you several times in the last several days. So now I'm asking you. Please. No wait- I'm telling you to put your ass in that chair and I mean now!"

The shocked look on Joe's face was priceless. Joe looked from Kay to the doctor then to the others before saying, "I'm okay. I feel great and I want to walk."

"Joe, honey," she pleaded. "Joe, please. If not for yourself, do it for me." A defiant look crossed Joe's face just as Kay continues,"Remember this guy is going to go play golf. I'll wait about twenty minutes before I break your leg and you'll sit here in pain for at least four hours before he's back. Now sit down and shut the hell up. Before I change my mind and break your damn fool neck."

Joe opened and closed his mouth several times before starting to point his finger, then slowly dropping his hand closing his mouth. Turning, he slowly dropped into the wheelchair. Looking at Kay, he starts to say something.

"Joe," she interrupted, "honey, I love you. I love you so very much. Now please just stop, you are not going to win this! I'm not kidding, Joe."

Joe met her eyes. When saw the pain in them, he quietly complied.

Adrian, Colton, and Chance quietly and quickly turned to leave, all laughing as Chance asked, "Are you sure that's Randy Jackson? He surely backed down in a hurry."

Adrian and Colton said at the same time, "Do you want to tangle with her?"

At the name of Randy Jackson, Doctor Diaz's head snapped to watch Adrian, Colton, and Chance as they left the room. Then looking at Joe, he quietly thought, *Randy Jackson? Randy Jackson? Oh my god. Can he be the ghost from Afghanistan? That was so many years ago.* Looking at Joe carefully, he thought, *He's had some work done. Although I did see several scars. It is, he's Commander Randy Jackson.* Looking at his signature he was puzzled, *Joe West?*

Joe watched as the doctor gave him the once over two or three times. He noticed when the doctor turned after Chance mentioned Randy Jackson. Now being in survival and protection mode, he carefully looked at Kay who had a questioning look on her face.

Chance glanced back over his shoulder laughing and said, "Not a chance. If Randy is scared of her then so am I. I wouldn't stand a chance.

Logan chuckled quietly. Joe turned to look. Logan stopped laughing and stood there, trying his best not to explode with laughter.

Rene had absolutely no control as she laughed so hard she started snorting. Clutching her stomach, she said, "I don't think I've ever seen him absolutely speechless."

That was all it took as Logan and Doctor Dias started laughing. Joe started to get up when Kay looked over at him. Seeing the look on her face, Joe simply dropped back into the chair, put his feet up and dropped his head waiting for everyone to get in control.

As they exited the hospital, Doctor Dias asked, "Where are you parked? I hope it's lot number three. I want this to continue as long as possible. I am so enjoying this. In the last couple of weeks, besides while he was unconscious, this is as quiet as he's ever been. He's not a bad patient, just too damn stubborn for his own good."

Kay replied, "Close, we are at the far end of the second lot."

Doctor Dias smiled. "Oh, that is absolutely perfect."

Joe started to raise himself out of the chair saying, "Oh, come on. I can walk. I am not an invalid."

Kay put her hand on Joe's shoulder and said, "Sweetheart, we are still at the hospital. Would you rather I just break it now? That way we won't have to go through admitting again? Now please, Joe, please sit there and enjoy the ride."

Arriving at Logan's pickup. Joe looked at the doctor and then his wife and asked, "Can I stand up now?"

Doctor Dias started to laugh then turned and looked at Kay. He asked, "What do you think? I'm sorry but everyone listens to you. I'm asking for your permission?"

Kay giggled. "Yes, honey, you can stand up but let someone help you."

"Help me? Like that's going to happen." Joe replied, as he started to rise out of the wheelchair.

As Joe stood, Doctor Dias stepped back and snapped to attention. Raising his right hand in a crisp salute, he said, "I was in Afghanistan several years ago. After hearing parts of your conversation I figure out who you are. I took a bullet out of your chest once before. I want to thank you for the service to your country Commander Randy Jackson. Call sign ghost."

With Doctor Dias standing at attention and saluting Joe, Logan, Adrian, Colton, and Chance all snapped to attention and saluted. Joe returned the salutes.

Looking from one to another Joe said, "I think we are going to find a place to hide for a few days. What are your plans?"

Adrian replied, "Colton and I are headed for Tucson. I think Chance is also. We all need to report what we have found out here. Then probably head back east. You have our numbers now. If you need us, just call. I still have enough pull to get a DEA jet and we can be wherever you are in a few hours." Looking at Chance he asked, "What are your plans?"

Chance replied, "Tucson today. Then I'll shadow Randy- I mean, Joe- as much as I can. We've already got something in place so I should be able to find him most anywhere."

Looking around, the handshakes and hugs started. Then stepping forward, Kay hugged each of the men that came to Joe's rescue. Then looking at Adrian, she said, "I have all of your numbers." Pausing, she looked back at her husband and said, "I'll call even if someone else won't."

Talking with doctor Dias a few more minutes, Kay climbed in the back seat of Logan's pickup. Joe looked at his military friends and said, "If it gets bad I'll call. I'll send Kay home with Logan and start hunting. The border doesn't bother me. I'm going to kill that fat Mexican. I want to give him these scars that he gave me several years ago."

As they left the hospital Logan said, "I've been working on your side-by-side. It was all shot to shit in the fight a few weeks ago. I think it would cost more to fix it than it would to replace it. I saw a dealership just up the road. Would you want to stop and look around?"

"Absolutely," Joe replied. "I really need to walk around." He smiled and looked at Kay and asked, "or do I need a wheelchair?"

Kay started to laugh as she said, "No, honey. We are away from the hospital now. So you can walk."

Joe glanced over at Kay who was looking at him. The look in her eyes tore at his heart. Slowly, the tears started to roll down her cheeks. He watched as one-by-one they increased to a steady stream. Reaching across the truck, he pulled her close as he whispered, "I love you, Kay. I love you so very much. There's absolutely nothing I wouldn't do for you."

Kay looked into the eyes of the man she loved and replied, "When you fell into my arms, I I thought you were-" she choked up through the words, "I thought you were dead. I tried to stop the bleeding but there was just too much. I cried the whole time you were in surgery. I thought I would die when the doctor said you had less than a fifty-fifty chance of surviving. I won't run Joe, and I'll do whatever you say. I know in my heart you'll die protecting me. You nearly did. Just promise me that'll you'll do what the doctor says until you are strong enough to be you again."

Joe had to pause for a moment. He knew his voice would break if he started talking. Slowly, he released her as he replied, "Yes, I'll follow his orders and do what you tell me. Although that fat Mexican is going to die. He knows who I am and I need to find him. If he gets to the Cartels…" Joe paused as his mind drifted back.

He was sitting in the shadows on a hillside overlooking the ocean, watching as several men unloaded two pickups into a waiting seaplane. Sending a coded message, he reported the tail number, color, description, and make of the plane to US authorities.

While watching, a message came back. Randy read the message several times. Shaking his head, he read it once again and thought, *They've gone nuts. There's absolutely no way I can survive this.* Then slowly, he read the message out loud again, "Stop the shipment. That plane and cargo cannot leave. Repeat, it cannot leave Columbia. Stop at all costs." Slowly, he typed: "Message received and understood."

Getting up, Randy turned and worked his way back into the jungle and across the hill while continuing to watch as they loaded the twin engine plane, trying to come up with some sort of a plan that he could live through.

As darkness fell it became clear that they were not planning on leaving until later that night or possibly morning.

Randy looked through his pack and found he only had a few grenades left. A five-second fuse meant he'd still be way too close when they went off. There was no way he could swim a safe distance along with the fact that the concussion could stun him if he was under water when they went off. Digging a little deeper, he found a black T-shirt and black running shorts. Thinking, he dropped over the back side of the hill and built a small fire. As the wood burned, he pulled several chunks out to cool. Making shadow lines across his arm and legs, he then covers his face with charcoal.

Watching from the jungle, he waited for darkness. Night was his friend. The Columbians had started to fear the darkness. His reputation had most of them staying inside or in groups at night. Slowly, he slipped down the hillside to the beach and into the water. As quietly as possible, he swam to the dock. Checking, he could see the guards all together sitting around a fire. Carefully, he came up under the plane. He quietly made his way into the shallows as he pulled the pin on one of the three remaining grenades.

Standing next to the tail, he threw the first towards the guards that were all still gathered around the fire. As it went off, he was on the dock and moving. Taking the second, he tossed it into the plane and ran as hard as possible towards the compound and the jungle beyond, screaming at the top of his lungs in Spanish, "It's the ghost! He's here! He's here, it's the ghost! Run for your lives! Take cover! It's the ghost!" Just as the plane exploded, he passed a building. Pulling the pin, he tossed the last through a window. A few seconds later the building exploded and was nearly totally engulfed in flames. Stopping just inside the safety of the jungle, he looked back at the carnage he had caused. Turning, he melted into the jungle.

Taking Kay by the hand, they walked over to a Bad Boy electric buggy. His mind was already several days ahead and his plan was coming together. After talking to the salesman, he headed for the service department. He was having them install a solar charging system and oversized gas tank along with gun scabbards. To the service department he said, "I'll come back tomorrow. Do you think it'll be ready?"

The service manager said, "Yes, it'll be ready by mid morning around 10:00."

Joe replied, "That'll be perfect. See you tomorrow."

Looking at Logan, he said, "I'm hungry. Let's get to the ranch, spend the night, and get the hell out of here tomorrow. I really want to go work on that gold claim for a few days before we have to head back. We can pick up that new wheeler in the morning on our way out."

CHAPTER TWELVE

Joe woke up and slipped out of bed. Careful not to wake Kay he poured a cup of coffee and walked out into the crisp desert air. A few minutes later he was looking over his new and very quiet ATV, reading the owner's manual. He sipped his morning coffee and enjoyed the quiet.

Glancing over, he watched as Logan walked out and looked around like he was lost. Seeing Joe, he slowly walked in that direction and said, "It's strange not to have the horses. I really wanted to work with Princess."

Joe replied, "Yeah, Kay is about half lost also. She hasn't said anything but I can see it in her eyes. She is always looking around like Midnight might just magically appear somewhere. I can tell she's missing him." Joe got up. "Come on, let's get breakfast started. I want to do some exploring around here and then head for that gold claim."

With breakfast done, Joe and Kay took the new Bad Boy while Logan and Rene used the Wild Cat. A few hours later they stopped at a desert water hole for a quick lunch before heading out again.

As they drove across the desert, Joe was looking for one thing- a trail taken by several vehicles in the last day or so. Seeing something that looked like it could be what he was looking for, he kept going before stopping a short distance away.

Looking at Kay, he said, "Nature calls. I have to pee." Then, glancing at Logan, he said, "I'll be right back." Joe walked the short distance and with his back to the others, he stood there looking at the tracks in the sand. Turning, he smiled at the rest as he walked back. He had found what he had been looking for. A track across the desert with more than five vehicles all going the same direction at a fairly high speed.

The rest of the day was spent exploring and sightseeing. As evening started getting closer, they found themselves back at camp. Joe had driven a fifty-mile circle and arrived back at the campers just before dark.

In the matter of a few minutes, he had a fire started and had found several nice big pieces of dry mesquite. Kay walked out with four thick cut rib-eyes along with four potatoes wrapped in foil. Joe placed the grill over the coals and added the mesquite, tossing the potatoes into the coals. Logan walked up with four bottles of beer. Handing two to Joe, he opened the other two, handing one to Rene as he dropped into a camp chair and said, "This is so peaceful. I could get used to this life, although I would need the horses."

Kay replied, "Yeah, I'm really missing Midnight. While Joe was in the hospital I barely thought about him. I sure am now."

Joe stuck the fork into one of the potatoes, then placed the four steaks on the grill. Sliding two off to one side, he left the other two over the flames for a few minutes. Turning them, he let them broil, searing in the juices and sliding them down. Moving the other two in their place and taking a fork, he rolled the potatoes around and twenty minutes later they sat down to a fantastic campfire-cooked meal.

With everything cleaned up Joe got up and walked into the camper. He came out with four more bottles of beer and the four friends sat talking about the gold claim. Joe noticed that no one said a thing about Hector or what had happened just a few weeks before. Joe was absolutely sure Hector was still in the area. He would not leave without trying to get Kay at least one more time and that would be his downfall. Joe wasn't about to let that happen. Not as long as he is still breathing. As they finished their beer, Logan got four more. Joe could tell that after four Kay was starting to feel the effect. That was perfect. Tonight was the night.

Just before midnight, Joe's eyes opened. He could feel Kay laying next to him. She was out cold. Rolling over, he kissed her cheek and said, "God willing, I'll be back before you wake up." Quietly, he slipped out of bed and was quickly dressed. Picking up the AR15 and several loaded magazines, then grabbing his belt with pistol and knife, he then slipped out the door. The Bad Boy whispered quietly as he slipped away on electric drive before starting the motor about a mile away.

Just over an hour later Joe was sitting on the top of a rise, looking down at a camp full of drug running, human trafficking scum. Joe continued to watch as everyone headed for their tents. Slipping through the shadows quietly as the wind, he made his way through the camp to the tents. His razor sharp knife opened the back without a sound. He quickly looked in each tent until he found what he was looking for. Joe had a pocket full of bullets. Picking up a rifle, he pushed a bullet into the barrel. Then he took a nail and a dead blow hammer and forced the bullets down the barrel. After doing all he could, he continued his late night visit. Moving and rearranging everything he could find. Then he slipped over to their Jeeps. Taking out his knife and the dead blow hammer, he cut little leaks in every radiator. Just as he finished, he heard voices and movement. Quickly, he was up and out of the camp. Carefully, he made his way back to where his ATV was hidden.

Just as he got into the ATV he heard yelling and screaming coming from the camp. Leaving on electric drive, he put a few miles between him and the gang of slime balls before starting the engine and driving as fast as he dared back to where they were camped.

Walking inside, he saw Kay standing there with a very disgusted look on her face. She yelled, "Just where in the hell have you been?! I woke up at about three and you weren't here! I looked all over the camp. I even woke up Logan. He's out with the other ATV trying to find you. Damn it Joe, you're not strong enough yet. Now where were you and don't try to soft talk me. I'm really not in the mood for it."

Pausing, Joe thought for a few seconds. He knew he couldn't and wouldn't try to cover it up. Pouring two cups of coffee, he handed one to Kay and said, "Sit down, and I'll tell you everything."

Pausing while he took a sip, he said, "I went and paid our Mexican friends a visit. I'm hoping I put enough fear into them that they'll leave, or at least leave us alone. The camp started waking up so I had to leave fast. Don't worry, I didn't get caught or seen. Although they'll know I was there. It worked in Montana. Hopefully it'll work again."

Kay stood up and screamed, "Are you kidding?! I'm not going to sit here every night wondering if you'll sneak off again! I thought you were dead when you fell into my arms at the ranch! I cried for days while you laid in the hospital fighting for your life! I'm not going to watch you die, Joe. I can't take that. I would rather leave you or, better yet, you leave. I mean now take what you want and go. I'll find a way back to Montana and then to Chicago. I'm done, you hear me. I'm fucking done."

Joe stood up and poured his cup into the sink. He turned and picked up Kay. Kicking the camper door open, he carried her outside. All the while she was kicking and screaming, "Put me down! Have you lost your mind? Put me down and I mean now!"

Joe carried her a short distance farther then let her slip to her feet. He said, "Look around. Look at that camper, the pickup. Think about everything we have at home in Montana. All of this and all of that doesn't mean a thing to me. None of it is worth having if I don't have you. You are all I want. All I've ever wanted. You are the reason I breathe. You are the reason I'm alive. I would have given up years ago. I just knew that somewhere, someone was waiting. That someone was looking for me. Someone that would give me a reason to live, to survive. Our meeting and marriage wasn't by accident. We were meant to be together. We were meant to find each other. We were meant to fall in love. I've been through more than any man alive. I've been shot, stabbed, tortured, and yet I'm alive. I should have died in Afghanistan or Columbia. But I didn't because I knew that somewhere someone would find me and give me a reason to live. Or I would find that someone. My god, Kay, look at us. We have ended each other's sentences. We have answered questions without the question ever being asked. Just a look and we know what the other is thinking. Our first kiss told the story. The way we melted into each other. We both knew at that point. This is real, we are real, and our love is meant to be."

Kay stood there with tears pouring out of her eyes as Joe walked forward and wrapped his arms around her. She forced her way back and started beating on his chest screaming, "I won't wait and worry just to find out you're dead somewhere! Please, that's the one thing I can't do. I love you as much as you love me. I'll go anywhere and do anything you ask of me. I'll follow you to the end of the world. I'll fight at your side. I would walk through hell carrying a case of dynamite for you. But I won't and I can't worry about you doing something like this ever again."

Joe stood, holding Kay as she melted into his chest sobbing. Looking around, he watched as Logan and Rene drove back into camp. Through the tears, Kay continued to sob, "I can't, I won't. Please Joe please I can't, I can't." As she started to compose herself, Logan asked, "Would you like to tell me just where you've been?"

Joe replied, "Not now, later. Okay, later."

Kay said, "He was out being the ghost. He paid a visit to the people trying to kill us."

Logan looked at Joe and said, "Is she kidding? Did you really go there? What the hell is wrong with you?"

Joe looked at his friend and said, "I did what I did." Pointing at Logan and Rene, he said, "Because of you and you." Then, looking at Kay, he said, "But mostly because of you."

Still looking into Kay's beautiful eyes, he continued, "I made a promise to you. A promise I'll never forget. I promised to always protect you. As long as I can breathe. As long as there's a spark of life in me. I'll keep that promise and if necessary I'll die protecting you. I'll spend eternity in hell just to make sure you are safe here and now."

Looking around, Joe walked to the fire. Staring into the flames, he said, "All I want is your love. It's all I've ever wanted. There's absolutely nothing I wouldn't do for you." Pausing, he turned and, through tear filled eyes, he looked at Kay and continued, "Never in my life have I felt this way. I prayed for a woman like you. Although I never dreamt my prayers would come true. I've seen you in my dreams both night and day. That day in Chicago when I told you everything I could about who and what I am, you sent me away. I laid there trying to decide if I could protect you. Somehow I knew this day would come. That my cover would be blown once again and something terrible would happen. Something to you," he said as he pointed at Kay. Continuing, he added, "Now I've gotten you and you involved in this." He pointed at both Logan and Rene.

Logan looked at Rene, Kay, and then at Joe and said, "We got involved a long time ago when we came to Mexico. I'll let you in on a little secret, my friend. I would do the exact same thing all over again. It's what friends do. So don't ever think I or we are upset about it."

Logan reached over, taking Rene's hand as he then walked forward and wrapped his arm around Rene and Kay. Kay put her arms around Logan and Joe as Joe put his arms around Kay and Rene. The four friends make their circle and pledged to always be there for each other.

Joe walked into the camper, lifting the bed and removing all the ammunition. Then pressing a button, another compartment opened. Reaching in, he took out two fully functional M-16s. Slipping full magazines into each, he looked at the selector, making sure it was safe. Walking towards Logan, he said, "This is going to get bloody I'm afraid. Here, take this and find a place for it. Make sure it's always available." He handed one to him.

Then looking at Kay and Rene he continued, "That's a fully functional M16 in Vietnam, in the north Viet Cong call it Black Death. Now we need to get ready. That means load every gun, every magazine, and put them in the pickups, campers, and ATVs. Anyplace you can think of. Make sure one is always closed. Oh, and never go anywhere without your pistol."

Joe then looked at Logan and Rene as his eyes drifted to Kay. He asked, "So, are we running or should we go to the gold claim? We can be there later today. It's still early and I did kick a big hornet's nest. If we leave as soon as possible, maybe they'll have trouble finding us again."

Pausing, he turned and looked back down the trail towards where the slime balls were camped and said, "That fat prick Pablo." Opening his shirt, he continued, "He gave me these, plus the ones on my back. If I ever see him again, I'm going to give him one." He slowly drew his finger across his throat.

Logan looked at Rene and asked, "Run, or finish our vacation time looking for gold?"

Rene smiled then started to giggle as she lifted her left hand and said, "Next to diamonds, gold is a girl's best friend."

Thirty minutes later, with everything loaded, the two pickups and campers left the campsite. Getting to the highway, Joe turned right and headed towards another town. Just outside of town he turned into a large truck stop, finding a parking place with room for Logan next to him. Walking to Logan's pickup he said, "Let's stay here for a few hours. After dark we'll look like just another truck leaving. If anyone is watching they'll have a hard time picking us out. Then let's go to Tucson for a few days before heading back into the desert. I would really like to take Kay to a nice relaxing restaurant."

Logan looked at Rene who said, "Let them go to the restaurant. I'll make you supper in bed."

Three hours later, under the cover of darkness, Joe pulled out onto the interstate and headed southeast for Tucson. Just after sunrise and about ten miles north of Tucson, he saw an RV park. Not having the horses, Joe pulled in and walked to the office where he paid for two spots for two nights. Walking back to Logan, he said, "Follow me, I have two spots all paid for." Finding their spots, they soon had power and water hooked up and both guys drained the sewage tanks. Leaving the hoses hooked up, they were set for a couple of days of pure relaxation.

Joe grabbed a couple of camp chairs and looked around to see the wood pile. Grabbing two bundles, he headed back to the camping spot and in a few minutes he had a nice little fire started.

Logan walked out a few minutes later. Sitting down, he handed a beer to Joe and asked, "How far is it to where we are headed?"

Joe took a couple of swallows and replied, "Oh, about a hundred miles. Maybe a little more. I have it marked on my GPS in the pickup. I'm thinking we can camp right at the sight."

Morning broke cool and crystal clear. Joe was up with coffee brewing as the eastern sky started to change colors. He sat in a camp chair and stared into the fire he had already started. Picking up the coffee pot, he filled his cup as Logan walked out of his camper with fresh sweet rolls.

Looking at Joe he said, "I'll trade you one of these for a cup of that coffee."

Chuckling, Joe filled one of the cups he had brought outside as Logan handed him a roll. It was hot and fresh from the oven, with butter already melting and dripping onto the small plate. A few minutes later both camper doors opened at the same time as Kay and Rene both walked out looking for coffee. Joe poured two more cups as Logan handed each of them a sweet roll.

Kay smiled as she took her first sip. "Wow, I could really get used to this."

Saying nothing, Rene sipped her coffee while chewing on the first bite. She enjoyed the beauty of the desert sunrise as the sky slowly turned from pink to red then blue.

Logan stood up and walked in a circle. He sat back down and picked up his coffee. He filled the cup and said, "I keep forgetting we don't have horses. I've had to feed and take care of horses every day of my life. This is so different and I'm still messed up."

Joe looked at Kay and said, "Happy anniversary, honey."

Kay smiled and said, "Oh my god. That's right, today. With everything that has happened I actually forgot."

Joe smiled and said, "I didn't. There's a really nice steak house in town and tonight I'm taking you out for dinner. If I remember correctly it's the same type as our first date."

Smiling, Kay replied, "Oh, you mean a coffee and ice cream store?"

Joe replied, "Honey, we went out to supper and then a nice walk on the beach on our first date."

She shook her head. "We met at a coffee and ice cream shop on our first date. We went out for dinner and walked on the beach on our second date."

Joe smiled and said, "We met at the ice cream store to talk and make plans for getting together again. Our first real date was when we went out to dinner. We had such a great time that night. It looked like an absolutely beautiful night. After dinner I didn't want to take you home. I couldn't think of anything to do. That's when I asked if you wanted to walk on the beach. All I could think of was spending as much time as possible with you. I couldn't believe you were actually with me. I fell in love with you that night. You got inside that wall I had around my heart that night. Even if you tell me to go away, I don't think I could ever get you out."

Looking at Kay, Joe watched a tear form and slowly slip from her eye. One after another, they slowly slipped down her cheeks. Kay blinked a few times and wiped her eyes as she stood up, bent down, and said, "You can be the biggest ass one moment and the sweetest man on earth the next." Kissing him, she said, "I need a shower." Looking over her shoulder as she walked away, "Ice cream store was the first date. Dinner and the walk on the beach was the second and yes, I melted into you on the first kiss. We stood outside next to my car and when you lifted my chin and kissed me." Smiling, she opened the camper door and walked inside.

Rene looked at Joe and said, "You really took her to an ice cream and coffee shop? My god, couldn't you come up with something a little nicer? Say a bit more romantic."

Joe replied, "I was surprised she called me. I think I was in shock. She had to be the most beautiful woman I had ever met."

Joe looked from Logan to Rene and said, "I think I'm the one that melted. I would have stood there and kissed her all night. I really didn't want that night to ever end. I know by the time I got to my room I had already fallen in love with her."

Looking at Rene, and then Joe, Logan said, "It took a herd of stampeding buffalo for me to realize I was in love with Rene."

Rene smiled. "Yes, if it wasn't for you and the speed of CJ, I wouldn't be here now."

Joe replied, "We all have an amazing past in one way or another. As soon as Kay's out of the shower she wants to do some shopping. I think we are going to go to Tucson."

Logan looked at Rene and said, "We should probably go to town also. We need to get groceries and ammunition. I looked last night and we are getting low on both."

"I can be ready in an hour or less," Rene confirmed.

True to her word, two hours later they headed for town to get groceries plus anything else they thought they might need for a month-long stay in the desert.

Joe's first stop was a sporting goods store, where he left with over a hundred boxes of ammunition. Glancing at Logan he asked, "Did you get enough?"

Logan replied, "I think I bought everything that you left. They didn't have any .223 or 5.56 left when I was done. I'm sure they are also out of 9MM and .45APC. I also grabbed twenty boxes of .308 and another twenty boxes of .22/250."

Joe smiled as he replied, "I've got thirty boxes of .22/250 already, plus at least twenty boxes of .308."

Looking across the parking lot, they watched as Kay and Rene pushed shopping carts overflowing with groceries their way. Looking at Joe, Logan said, "I'm thinking we won't be having lunch in town. Those carts are full, that means we'll need to get them put away."

Smiling, Joe replied, "Yep, two piles. One for inside and another to go to the storage boxes and put into the compartments under the campers."

Arriving back at the campers, it took nearly an hour to get everything put away. Kay called out, "Joe, I'm going to get a shower before we go. I'll be ready in an hour or so."

Joe was waiting in the kitchen drinking coffee. He was dressed in a gray sports coat and black dress pants along with his black boots and new black stetson.

Kay walked out in a off the shoulder black dress that was just a couple of inches short of hitting the floor. Her right leg came through the split up the side as she walked. Standing up, Joe watched as she came towards him. Kay asked, "Joe, is something wrong?" as she did a quick check of her dress to make sure everything was closed and buttoned.

Joe finally answered, "Everything is fine. I haven't seen you dressed up in a long time. I can't believe how beautiful you are."

Bowing, he offered his arm as he said, "Honey, you look absolutely stunning." Opening the camper door, Joe walked down the steps. Then he turned and held her hand as Kay walked out.

Logan and Rene were already outside as Joe and Kay came out of their trailer. With everything ready, they headed for a night on the town.

Joe's eyes snapped open just before five. Rolling over, he put his arm around Kay and laid there, enjoying the closeness of his wife. Kissing her, he then carefully slipped out of bed, making coffee as he walked outside to watch the desert come alive.

Joe finished the first pot and was refilling the craft as Logan walked out. Sitting down, he sipped his first cup as Joe walked out of the camper. Smiling, Joe said, "It's about time you get up. I've been out here for nearly an hour. There's a nice little pond back there a couple hundred yards with a small beach. I think it's spring fed. The water is crystal clear and still cool this morning. Although I'm sure it'll be nice and warm by early afternoon."

Logan replied, "Wow, sweet. Come on, let's go for a walk. I'm stiff this morning. I think Rene is trying to kill me."

Joe chuckled as he got up and followed Logan. He said, "She must be related to Kay. After me being an idiot yesterday and our little fight. Let's just say I'm still trying to walk off cramps in certain muscles and I've been up longer than you."

Walking around the pond, Logan said, "I'm sure Rene and I will be back here to cool off later today."

Joe removed his boots and socks. Rolling up his pants, he walked in a few feet and said, "Oh wow, this feels fantastic. Yeah I'm sure Kay and I will be also."

They continued to talk and look at the surrounding desert as they headed back to the campers. Arriving back to where they were parked, Kay and Rene were both sitting at the table enjoying the cool fresh air of the morning desert before the heat later in the day forced them inside. Watching as their husbands walked back into view, Kay said, "Well at least I know he's not out trying to piss me off again."

Logan said, "Morning, ladies!"

Rene asked, "What have you two been up to?"

Joe replied, "Just looking around some." Turning around, he pointed at the trees that surrounded the small pool as he continued, "There's a really nice spring feed little pool back there. The water is cool and crystal clear."

"My god, that sounds awesome," Kay sighed

Joe bowed as he reached out and took her hand. He asked, "Would you like a personal tour?"

Logan filled all four coffee cups and snickered as he reached for Rene's hand whispering, "I think Kay is still just a little mad at him. Maybe we should be escorts and possibly act as a referee."

Rene replied, "I know she's still upset. Although I also know she loves him as much as he loves her. They really do make the perfect couple. There's absolutely nothing they wouldn't do for each other."

Joe placed his hand low on Kay's back as he directed her in front of him and walked at her side just a half step behind. His eyes continuously scanned the area as all four walked towards the trees and the hidden desert pool.

Coming around the corner, the area around the pools opened up. Kay stopped and looked at Joe. She smiled and said "This kind of reminds me of that little pool we found a few years ago in the mountains."

Joe grinned as his mind drifted back and he remembered the little desert oasis and what had happened on that beautiful afternoon. His mind continued to relive that trip. It should have been just a simple mountain lion relocation, but ended up being a fight-and-flight for their lives from a deranged mad man after he kidnapped Kay. Joe had no choice but to contact Logan and ask for help. Now nearly three years later and it was still happening. Hector and Juan just wouldn't go away. To make things worse, Pablo was here helping to set things up to get more cocaine transported into the US and had recognized Joe from years ago.

Kay reached over, taking Joe's hand she pulled him closer and said, "Oh, I think we need to come back here later today or maybe tonight and spend some alone time."

Joe's smile grew as he invisions alone time with Kay later that evening, relaxing around the beautiful little pool. Continuing around the pool Joe put his arm around Kay and pulled her closer. She laid her head against his shoulder and they continued to walk around the pool and back to the campers.

Filling the coffee cups again, they all sat down at a picnic table and discussed what that day's plans were.

A couple hours later Joe was working on the Wild Cat when saw he needed a few new parts. Calling to Kay, he said, "I have to run and get a few things. I shouldn't be gone more than an hour or so. Do you want to come with me or do you need me to pick you up anything?"

"No hon, I'm good," she replied. "I'm going to make a couple of salads for supper and just relax today."

Joe walked in and gave her a kiss, grabbing the keys and heading for town.

After getting all the parts he needed, he headed back in less than an hour. Arriving back at the camper, he walked into the camper calling for Kay. When there was no answer, he walked over to Logans and asked, "Have you seen Kay? She's not in the camper or anywhere around here that I can find."

Rene replied, "I talked to her about fifteen minutes ago. She said something about walking down by that little pool."

Joe walked back to the camper. Grabbing his Glock 26, he checked the suppressor, making sure it was tight. He slipped it into his jacket pocket as he walked towards the trail leading to the pool. Just as he cleared the last of the trees, he heard Kay scream, "No get away! Leave me alone. No! No! I said leave me alone.

Joe came around the last turn in the trail to see a man with a knife threatening Kay. He hollered, "She said to leave her alone. Now I'm telling you to leave her alone and get out of here before I get pissed and you get hurt." The man grabbed Kay by the hair. He pulled her head back and put the knife to her throat. He yanked her in front of him with his head on her left side. Joe's hand came out of his pocket with the Glock in a two handed grip as he continued to threaten him, "Let her go and walk away. I promise I won't hurt you. If you hurt her so much as a scratch you'll regret ever coming here."

Joe continued to talk and worked his way closer. He was thirty feet away. Although he knew he could hit him at this range, if he pulled the shot just a little the bullet could hit Kay. It was simply too far plus there was the problem that he was left-handed and the man's head was on Kay's left side. With the knife in his right hand, one of three things would happen when he pulled the trigger: the man would die instantly, letting go of the knife and falling over backwards, or his hand would grip the knife tight, pulling it through Kay's throat as he fell back. The third was the worst. He could pull the shot and kill his wife.

He had to get the guy to move his head to Kay's right. This way it would totally eliminate one of the three possibilities. If Joe pulled the shot it would simply move the bullet to the left away from Kay. Also, if he gripped the knife tighter as he fell back, there was a chance he wouldn't cut her throat because he would be falling straight back and not with his arm being drawn at an angle.

Joe kept working his way to Kay's right, trying to get the man to move his head. As Joe spoke, he took a step to his left or Kay's right. This way he was moving out of the man's line of sight. Remaining calm, he told the guy over and over to let her go and walk away. Joe kept talking and working his way to his left. He could see the terrified look in Kay's eyes. He could see the tears as they formed and ran down her cheeks. He could hear the sobs as she felt the knife against her throat.

Although worse of all was the look in her eyes. The look of sheer terror that begged him to help her. The look that tore at his heart and told him not to fail because he had to save her. Nothing else mattered at that time. All of his training came into play. It all came down to one shot. The shot he had trained for, his entire life. The shot that would dictate the rest of his life. The shot that would save Kay's life.

Joe stopped moving; he focused on the front sight, rear sight and then the man's eyes. Again Joe said, "Let her go and live. Hurt her and die." The man's hand tightened on the knife and Joe's finger slowly squeezed the trigger. The pistol made a little pop as the 147 grain subsonic bullet passed within three inches of Kay's ear, striking the man just above his right eye. As he fell backwards, his hand pulled Kay to the left and the knife fell away to her right side.

Kay screamed as the angry buzz of the bullet passed within three inches of her right ear. In six quick steps, Joe had Kay wrapped in his arms as she continued to scream in sheer terror.

Slowly, he rocked her from side to side as he stroked hair, working her in a half circle until the dead man was lying behind her. Then lifting her up, he whispered, "I've got you honey. I've got you. It's over hon. I've got you." Joe continued to stroke her hair and scan the area as he carried her back to the campers, Logan, Rene, and safety.

Looking at Logan, he said, "Get us ready to leave as soon as humanly possible."

Logan gave him a funny look and said, "What's up?"

Joe replied, "Just get us ready. I'll be back in a few minutes. I have to take care of something."

Logan looked at Rene and said, "He is acting really strange."

Kay replied, "I think Hector may know we are here. I was just attacked and Joe killed him. I think he's going to hide the body and try to give us a head start before the authorities find it."

Logan swore as his hand went inside the light shirt he had on over a t-shirt and said, "You two get in the pickups. I'll get them both hooked up. As soon as he's back we are out of here. Joe says it's about two hours, maybe a shade more to where we are going. I want to be out of here as soon as he's back."

Joe went back to where the body was and saw there was a slight problem. The body was gone. Looking around he saw what looked like watered down blood and a few pieces of what could be fragments of skull. Glancing around at the surrounding area, he saw his shell casing laying just a few feet away. Picking it up, he continued to look at the surrounding area until he saw a dimple in a tree. Walking up, he looked carefully and in a few minutes he carved around and found the bullet. Using his leatherman handy tool, he worked it out of the tree and fifteen minutes later he was walking back into camp. Jumping out of the pickup, Kay ran to him as Joe wrapped her in a tight secure hug. Slowly and ever so tenderly he held her, stroking her hair and kissing the top of her head, slowly working his way to her forehead and then lips.

Looking at Logan he asked, "Are we ready? I really want to get the hell out of here."

Logan replied, "I'm following you, so let's go. Everything is loaded, hooked up, and ready." Glancing around, he helped Kay get inside. Pulling onto the highway, Joe headed north, looking for a truck stop to hide for an hour or so before heading back into the desert and to the gold claim.

Arriving at a truck stop, Joe reached into the back seat. Kay watched as he slipped on a denim jacket. She knew what that jacket was and what it meant. Under Joe's right arm was a carefully tailored holster designed to fit his suppressed Glock. Under his left arm were five precisely balanced razor sharp throwing knives.

Kay looked at Joe and she could tell he was in full protection mode. His eyes continuously scanned the area as they walked inside. Glancing at Logan, she could see the bulge in his coat. She knew that the huge .44 magnum was hanging in a shoulder holster under his left arm.

Joe saw the table he wanted. Placing his hand on Kay's back, he carefully steered her through the restaurant to the table. Pulling a chair out for Kay, he sat with his back against the wall as Logan and Rene joined them.

They were not seated as normal. With both Joe and Logan sitting in such a way, they could see every one that entered the restaurant and hopefully head off any trouble that may come their way.

In a few minutes, the waitress took their orders and slowly they all started to relax as they talked about what the next few days would hold. They discussed the gold claim and the equipment they have to get set up.

Joe continued to watch the door and everyone that entered as they ate. His eyes continued to shift from quadrant to quadrant as he talked about the claim. After finishing his meal, Joe pushed his plate away and filled his coffee cup once again. Slowly, his hand moved inside his coat and found the grip of his 9MM Glock 26. Knowing he had already checked the chamber, he watched as five guys walked in and stared in their direction.

Glancing at Logan, he moved his eyes over back and over again. Logan's hand slipped inside his jacket as Joe gave him a signal telling him to stand down. He then nodded at the bill on the table.

Logan picked up the bill and all four rose as one. With Logan leading, all four headed for the door with Joe bringing up the tail. With Logan, Rene and Kay standing at the register, Joe slipped off to the restroom. He exited the restroom a few minutes later with Logan already paying the bill and redirecting Kay and Rene ahead of him. They walked out with the five guys following. Joe followed the five guys.

As soon as they cleared the door, Logan pushed Kay and Rene into a corner and turned. He stood between them and the guys following.

Martin stepped forward and said, "Hector and Juan want those two women, cowboy. So step aside and you won't get hurt."

Joe took four rapid steps and pushed his way between the guys. Placing the barrel against his back he whispered, "Isn't that just too damn bad. We are not willing to let you or them have these women. Now if you are smart, which I'm not sure you are, you will simply turn and walk back inside before I pull the trigger and break your spine, paralyzing you from right about here down." He pushed the barrel harder into Martin's back.

Slowly, all five turned to look at Joe who smiled as he said, "Now prove you're not as dumb as you look and walk away. I've already killed one of your friends today and I really want to end this right here and now."

Martin looked at the man looking at him, then quickly to other four he said in Spanish, "I thought this gringo was smart. He doesn't impress me. Get ready. Hector and Juan are going to be very happy with us." Then changing to English, he said, "If I raise my arm, the other twenty guys will be here in a few seconds. You might be good but you can't kill all of us."

Joe smiled and answered in perfect Spanish, "You'll never know because you'll be the first one to die so go ahead raise your arm. I have fourteen shots in this clip and two more clips in my back pocket and Logan has six shots plus several speed loaders. I'm quite sure most of you, if not all, will die. Although it's like I said, you'll never know. You'll be the first one to die. So simply walk past me and don't look back. Because if you do, I'll put two in you before anyone else gets a chance to move. Then I'll kill everyone I can. At this range all five of you. Along with several of your friends if they try to help you. I'm sure Logan will kill at least five. I'm sure Kay and Rene are also armed. I'm sure they'll get a few each so out of twenty four, maybe there will be a few left to tell Hector and Juan you failed again. They won't survive that."

Martin looked around then back at Joe. What he saw unnerved him. The look in Joe's eyes had changed. It was the look of a man ready to fight and defend what was his. Martin knew this man would fight and die protecting the beautiful black haired lady standing behind the big cowboy. Ever so slowly Martin stepped to the side and carefully walked around Joe, followed by the other four.

Joe's hand came out of his pocket, still holding the Glock. Quickly, he turned and watched them all walk away. One quick glance over his shoulder and he saw as Kay took a step forward to stand next to him. With the pistol still in his left hand, his right went to Kay's back as he slowly directed her towards the pickup and camper parked a couple hundred feet away.

Joe helped Kay into the pickup. Then walking around the camper, he stopped next to Logan and said, "We are about two hours to where the road leads into the desert. Then it's at least an hour to where the claim is." Pausing, he looked around before turning back to Logan and said, "How in the hell do they always know where we are? I've watched our back trail and from what I can see, we are not being followed."

Getting a high power light, Joe started to inspect the pickup and trailer. Going over both a couple of times, he looked at Logan and said, "I can't find anything. Although I still think they are tracking us." Looking around the area, he continued, "Come on, let's go. I really want to get the hell out of here." A few minutes later they dropped into the interstate and headed in a north eastern direction.

Joe saw the road leading into the desert. Stopping a couple hundred feet in, he jumped out and quickly cut two pieces of brush covered with leaves. Handing one to Logan, he said, "Let's try and cover our trail." In a few minutes there was no trace that they exited the highway and headed into the desert.

Getting to the claim, they got the camp set up with the doors facing each other. Joe's pickup was poised to drive straight out into the desert while Logan's was closing off one end, leaving a space of about 15 feet between them and giving them some privacy and cover. Joe got out the fire ring then joined the others in gathering firewood. In the matter of an hour they had several days of firewood stacked and a nice fire going. Logan disappeared into the camper and walked out a few minutes later with four beers as the friends sat down to enjoy a pleasant desert evening.

After a few hours of light hearted conversation and some discussion of what the next couple of days might be like it was getting late. Logan looked at Rene then over at Joe and Kay before saying," Tomorrow is going to be a full day. I think I'm about done in." Taking Rene by the hand he continued," See you in the morning."

Joe focused on the front sight, then he brought the rear into place just as the man pulled the blade across Kay's neck. Kay tried to scream although all Joe heard was a sick gurgling sound. He watched as she dropped down onto her knees and then fell onto her face in the desert sand. As the sand mixed with a growing pool of her own blood. Joe's eyes snapped open and he jumped from bed screaming, "No! No! No!" with his hands up in a two handed grip, squeezing the trigger. Again he screamed, "No! You rotten son of a bitch!" Drenched in sweat and gasping for air, he had relived the scene of Kay being held with a knife to her throat in his dreams. Only this time the man cut her throat just before Joe had pulled the trigger.

Kay jumped when Joe screamed. She knew better than to get to him too quickly, although she saw his eyes were open and he was moving.

Slowly, she wrapped her arms around him. Holding him, she started rubbing his back and slowly stroking his hair, just as Joe had done for her so many times before.

Joe's breathing slowly returned to normal as he held onto Kay. Her body was so close and the warmth helped bring his nerves back to a normal state as he started to calm down.

Kay leaned back and looked at her husband. She asked, "My god, honey, are you ok? What on earth happened? Why are you shaking like this?"

Joe looked at her as he reached for a pair of sweats and a t-shirt and said, "Just another bad dream. Something like the others I've told you about. I'll be ok." Walking to the kitchen area of the camper, he started coffee and headed outside, stirring up the coals from the night before and adding a few smaller pieces he soon had a fire going.

The fire felt good in the cool morning air. Getting up, he walked back into the camper. He filled a carafe then made another pot before grabbing four cups and heading back outside. Looking around, he put the carafe and cups on the camp table before filling up a cup. Walking over to his new Bad Boy ATV, he took the AR15 out of its holder. Checking to make sure the magazine was full, he put it down on the tail gate of his pickup just five feet away.

Hearing the camper door, he watched as Kay walked out in her nightgown and robe. Sitting next to him, she placed her hand on his leg as Joe handed her a cup. Looking into his eyes, she pried, "Afghanistan, Columbia, or something else? I know you have dreamt about us dying in an accident or plane crash."

Joe paused, then took a sip and said, "Something else." Pausing for another sip, he continued, "You know I'll protect you with my life, but right now I really don't want to talk about it."

Kay smiled, leaned forward, and kissed him before saying, "Joe honey you have to talk about it. Get it out that way and deal with it."

With that million-mile stare in Joe's eyes, Kay said, "That dream really scared you. I've dealt with your nightmares and dreams for several years. Although there's something different with the way you are acting with this one. Please, hon. Please tell me what it was about. Please, so I can help you."

Joe took another sip of coffee and turned to look into Kay's beautiful eyes and said, "I screwed up. I waited too long."

Kay looked at Joe with a puzzled look on her face as she replied, "Screwed up? Waited too long? Joe, what are you talking about? You have an uncanny ability to judge what's about to happen, along with being able to think clearly under pressure." Pausing, she continued, "Waited too long for what?"

Joe looked down, then back AT Kay. With a tear slowly tracing a path down his cheek he said, "At the pond in Tucson. That guy with the knife. I waited too long. In my dream he, umm, he-" now the tears were a steady stream as he continued, "he cut your throat. Just before I pulled the trigger. With you in my sight picture I, umm, I was scared I'd pull the shot and everything was way too close. You were too close to my bullet path. I waited too long. Hell, it was only 20 feet. I could have hit him twenty times. I waited and put your life in more danger than I should have."

Kay turned slightly then wrapped her arms around him. She whispered, "You did exactly what was right. I am alive and unharmed. If you hadn't gotten there at that time only god knows where I would be right now."

Joe smiled as he lifted her chin and kissed her. He could feel himself melting into her as she melted against him. The kiss brought them together as one. One heart, one life, one love.

Logan walked up, followed a few minutes later by Rene. Pouring two cups, he sat down as he handed a cup to Rene and said, "What are the plans today? Are you going to try to find a way through that maze of tunnels or are we going in from above? I'm not sure how we can get that generator up there, let alone into that cavern without it getting wet."

Joe assured him, "I'll find a way through the tunnels. I'll also mark each and every turn so we can go back and forth."

Logan looked over at the generator and then up to the mountain and replied, "Good, I don't think even together we could get that generator up there."

Joe laughed and said, "Nope, just hire a helicopter."

Joe got up and in a few minutes he was ready. Grabbing several spools of life line, he parked one of the Wild Cats at the opening of the tunnel and tied one end. With two flashlights and a can of green water based paint, he headed into the tunnel.

Logan started getting everything ready. They would start hauling everything into the cavern as soon as Joe came back out- if he found a way into the underground lake. With everything in place except the generator, he watched as Kay and Rene started cleaning and rearranging the campers and camping area. Making sure there was a rifle available in every vehicle, and placed in different areas of their camp. With Hector and Juan still in the area, Kay and Rene stayed close to either Joe or Logan at all times.

High on a mountain side and a mile away, Santiago watched as the four friends sat up in the camp and waited for Joe to come out of the tunnel.

In Tucson, Chance opened his phone. Writing Joe's location down, he closed his phone and went back to work.

CHAPTER THIRTEEN

Joe emerged from the tunnel with all smiles as he said, "Made more than one wrong turn, but I found it. I marked the turns on the way out. Wow, what a maze that is." Looking at Kay, he continued, "I'm really happy that we didn't try and find our way out of there. I'm sure we would have gotten lost and would probably still be in that mess somewhere."

Logan asked, "How did you mark the way in?"

"Green dot means straight ahead. Green arrow tells you when to turn. It's marked both in and out on the right hand side. Simply follow the arrows of the arrow going forward and up the right turn. Forward and down left turn. and you'll get in and out. It's water based and will simply be washed away over time."

Rene asked, "When are we going to start hauling all this equipment inside?"

Joe replied, "No time like the present. Let's do it tomorrow. I'm beat, it's a long walk. I think a cold beer and a great supper is on my list."

Rene smiled. Looking at Logan she replied, "You get a fire going. While we were shopping I found some fantastic looking steaks. I just happen to have four laying on the counter."

Logan looked at Joe and said, "You heard the lady. We need a fire and that would be your job. I'll find us a couple bottles of ice cold beer."

Kay said, "I've got a salad all ready. How about potatoes? Pan fried or fire baked?"

Logan looked at Joe and said, "Either way works for me. How about you?"

"Whatever is the easiest," Joe shrugged.

"Get the fire started," said Kay. "We need hot coals. It's going to be fire baked."

In ten minutes Joe had a fire going. Then he joined Logan looking for firewood. In the matter of a half hour there were hot coals to start cooking on. Joe continued to add fast burning smaller branches to the fire. Using a small shovel, he scooped hot coals to the side while adding more wood.

Kay walked out a few minutes later with four potatoes all wrapped in foil. Joe placed them in the coals and scooped up another shovel full and covered the foil wrapped potatoes. Throwing in several nice chunks of mesquite, he watched as they burned. Sliding the grill into place, Joe stood up and walked into the camper. Grabbing a container of prime rib rub, he gave all four steaks a liberal coating on both sides. Place two on the grill, he gave them time to sear before turning them over and waiting a few minutes. Sliding them off to the side, he puts on the last two.

Twenty minutes later they enjoyed a fantastic supper cooked over a campfire. With everything cleaned up and put away, Joe came out with four bottles of beer. Opening the first two, he handed them to Logan and Rene. Opening the next two, he handed one to Kay before taking his seat next to her.

Just over a mile away, Santiago continued to watch as the day faded to darkness before heading for their camp to report what he had found. He knew that if Hector got Kay it would be an all out race for the border and home.

After a few more beers, the friends called it a night and headed for their campers for some private time.

He was lying on a mountain side watching as the Taliban fighter beat a man in a small village. They were hunting him and knew he was in the area from an attack a few nights before. He had carefully walked through their encampment and placed hand grenadines carefully in their supplies. That way whenever someone went looking hopefully him and a few others would make that one way trip. Plus the fact it would put fear into all of the rest. He sat a mile away and watched as four guys started looking through their stolen storage. He hated that the people were so poor and yet the Taliban just took what they wanted. If someone stood up to them, that person would either be beaten or shot. The young women were usually taken and either sold, killed, or abandoned after everyone had their fun with them.

Sitting there, he saw a flash before he heard the grenadines detonate. He watched as the four closest men were blown through the air, landing in a heap. He saw two others drop to the ground. Getting up, he started the long climb over the top and into another valley. He knew they'd be on his trail again soon enough.

Joe's eyes snapped open. Shaking in a cold sweat, he carefully scanned the area before moving. It took just a few seconds for him to realize it was just another dream. Rolling to his side he found Kay and carefully pulled her closer. The heat of her body brought a sense of peace to him, knowing he was somewhat safe and that she loved him gave him the strength to keep moving forward each and every day. It was only her love that kept him from going hunting and killing Hector and everyone with him. He couldn't take the chance that Hector would attack their camp while he was gone.

Joe slipped out of bed. Quietly, he got dressed and made coffee. Slipping outside, he watched as the eastern sky started to lighten. Sipping his coffee, he thought about Afghanistan and Columbia. He thought about his life before Kay and what he had survived. Hector now wanted to take the only person he had ever truly loved and cared about. He was sick of killing. He had done way too much already. Although in his heart and mind he knew that he would have to kill again and again. He would do whatever it took to protect Kay, Logan, and Rene. Walking over to his pickup, and grabbing his shoulder holster, he strapped on Kimber 1911 .45 and picked up his coffee as he walked back to the camper. Sitting down at the table, he sipped his coffee and enjoyed the quiet of the predawn.

Watching as Logan's camper door opened, Logan came walking out with a smile and an empty coffee cup. "Morning Logan," he said as he filled the cup. Logan mumbled something close to morning as he took that first sip. Shaking his head, he continued, "I have no idea what got into Rene, but I swear she's trying to kill me."

Joe snickered and said, "I'm quite sure there are a lot of guys who would love to be in your place. Although yes, I feel for you. Kay has been so very nice to me lately."

Joe looked up as he heard the camper door close and Kay said, "And as long as you don't try and sneak off again, I'll continue to be nice to you. Now since I was so nice last night, would you please pour me a cup of that coffee? I heard Logan so I started frying bacon and I'm sure Rene will be here soon."

A few minutes later Rene walked out of their camper with a cup, a smile, and an old fashioned coffee pot. Placing it on the cooking rack but off to the side slightly, she joined the others and watched the eastern sky turn a vivid blue.

Joe threw several more pieces of wood on the fire as Kay came back out of the camper with a frying pan full of sliced potatoes. Placing it on the rack, she sat down again and took up her cup saying, "Breakfast will be ready in about thirty minutes. With that partially cooked bacon in with the potatoes." It had only been a few minutes but the aroma of bacon frying invaded everyone's senses.

As one, they started to wake up. Kay got up one more time. Going into the camper, she came out twenty minutes later dressed and with a dozen eggs already scrambled and poured it in with the potatoes and bacon. There were also green and red peppers and a diced up onion. Mixing everything together, she picked up a plate and dished up what she called gold claim surprise.

With all the equipment ready, Joe and Kay took the first trip into the underground that would lead them to an underground paradise.

A lake, small trees, and grass- not to mention gold. As they exited the tunnel it was Logan and Rene's turn. A few hours later they came walking out. All either could do was smile. Logan looked at Joe and said, "That has to be one of the richest gold gains I've ever seen or even heard about. If we work in pairs, leaving two out here to watch for trouble, we can probably bag several ounces a week. Let's say we work it for two weeks. We should have several thousand dollars. I don't need the money and I don't think you do. So let's just bag it and let it set until we do. We can always come back next year and do the same thing and just bank roll it. We both have safes at home."

Joe agreed and said, "Come on, hon, it's our turn. We can take in the last trip and work the claim for a couple of hours. By then it'll be getting dark and they can work the first shift in the morning."

Arriving at the sight, Kay walked into the water and said, "Wow, this feels fantastic." Walking in a little deeper, she washed off the dust and sweat from the walk in. Joe got the gold sluice set up.

Sticking a shovel at the low end and handing Kay a two gallon pail, he said, "I'll bring the sand from over by the wall to you and pour it in this end. You can pour water on it, washing it down the sluice. If I have the angle right, the gold should get caught behind those cross bars while the lighter sand and rocks wash out that end. Use the shovel to keep that end somewhat open so it doesn't back up the sluice."

After a couple of hours hauling two buckets at a time, Joe was absolutely exhausted. Walking into the underground lake, he fell forward and cooled off. Kay watched and slowly walked out to where he was floating. Bringing his feet back under him, he stood up and reached for her. Smiling, she kissed him and said, "Let's call it a day. We can do more tomorrow. Do we bring anything out with us?"

Joe replied, "No, I think we can leave everything pretty much where it is. I'll tell Logan what we did. They can do the same or maybe figure out something else."

Just as they reached the end of the tunnel, Joe stopped. Listening carefully, he walked over and picked up two rifles from a large pile of rocks. Working the action, he handed one to Kay and said, "I put these there just before Logan and Rene came out. I want to make sure we had something just in case. Better to be safe than to be sorry."

Walking out into the open, Logan stood up and called out, "I didn't think you would ever come out. We have been waiting and watching for you. Rene has supper nearly done." He walked over and he got four bottles of beer, opening the first two and handing them to Joe and Kay "Go sit down. You look exhausted. I'll bring supper to you."

Just then Rene walked out of the camper with two plates all dished up. Handing them to Logan, she said, "Here, I'll be right back with ours."

As they sat enjoying supper, Joe told Logan and Rene about what Kay and himself had sat up and how it worked. Logan replied, "That sounds pretty easy. I think we'll do the same thing. Only Rene can haul from the wall."

Rene laughed as she nearly spit out a mouthful of food and said, "Maybe two or three trips, then that'll be your job. I get to stand in the water and stay cool while you haul it."

Kay spoke up saying, "Neither job is easy. Joe kept me plenty busy. It takes several buckets of water to keep up. There were a few times he got back before I had the sluice ready for more."

With supper finished and everything cleaned up, Joe and Logan walked around the campsite, making sure everything was picked up and put away, except for what they were currently using. Picking up two huge arm loads of firewood, they walked back to camp. Placing the wood with the rest they had gathered earlier, Joe grabbed four bottles of beer before sitting down with the others.

Talking more about the sluice and how easy it had worked, Logan asked, "Did you notice if there was any gold in it?"

Smiling Joe replied, "Yes sir, I could see a lot of color. I was tempted to do a clean out, although I thought it would be a whole lot easier if there was a lot of gold so we could do one tomorrow afternoon. Whoever goes in last can take that small cooler, put in the carpet plus whatever sand is in it. They can use a bucket to remove as much water as possible. Then carry it out, we can all watch as we pan it out."

Joe looked around and said, "If we take a good gold pan. Say one of the new ones. Then carefully pan out what comes out of the sluice on the last trip of each day. We should have several ounces of gold in a week or so."

Just as they finished eating, a coffee cup exploded, showering them in coffee and pieces of flying ceramic. Joe tipped the table over, knocking Logan and Rene to the ground as he grabbed for Kay, tipping over her chair. He came up with a pistol in his hand.

Joe yelled, "Kay, run!" Instead of running away, Joe ran at the men charging the camp with a knife in one hand and his .45 in the other. He met the charge with deadly force, dropping to one knee and opening fire. He killed the first four guys with two or three shots each in the center of their chest. The men kept running towards their camp. Spinning, he knifed the next as he swung his left hand with the pistol into the side of another's head, knocking him to the ground. With several down, a shot rang out from behind, killing the next one as Logan charged into the free for all. Hitting the group of men like a wild bull, he screamed, "You bunch of low life assholes!"

He then picked up the next one up by the throat and crouched. He literally threw him into the rest. Looking around, he saw more coming and yelled to Joe, "Come on, let's get out of here."

Logan ran over a small hill as Joe spun to meet the newcomers. Firing two shots, he killed one and wounded another. Placing his thumb on the magazine release and snapping his wrist, he let the empty magazine fall to the ground as he pushed in a full magazine. Moving his thumb to the slide release, he was hit from behind, dropping to his knees and falling forward into the desert sand and slowly slid down a long tunnel into darkness.

Kay knew she was seriously outgunned. She had no idea where Logan and Rene were or if they were even still alive.

Hector and his gang executed a perfect raid and separated the four friends. Kay managed to grab a rifle and a small pack as she ran for cover. The pack held a couple of clips and two boxes of shells. Her .22/250 was flat shooting and deadly accurate.

As the gang of claim jumping, drug running, human trafficking slime balls charged into camp, Joe yelled for everyone to run, but instead of running, Joe attacked which gave the others a chance.

Kay continued to move the scope from target to target. Suddenly, she saw a flash of light coming from something or someone above and beyond where Joe was being held.

Hector drew back and punched Joe in the kidneys, dropping him to his knees, just as a shot rang out. She watched as Juan grabbed his shoulder and then dropped from sight. Kay's finger tightened on the trigger as Hector ran for cover. Forgetting momentarily about Joe laying just a few feet away, she slowly squeezes the trigger.

Kay's shot was off a couple of inches as the bullet hit him in the upper shoulder instead of the center of his chest. He had started turning and dropping just as the gun went off. That and that alone had saved his life. Kay was pissed beyond belief and had absolutely no patience left. She slowly moved the crosshairs away from Joe as she scanned the area. With his hands tied behind his back, there was no way he could protect himself.

She knew Hector would kill him if she fired or showed herself. It was only two hundred yards, but Hector was way too close to Joe, thus putting Joe continuously in the sight picture. She knew the light bullet could drift just a few inches. In that case she could or would hit Joe.

A smile came to her face as she saw Logan rise from behind a clump of brush. She watched as he carefully crawled forward, trying to get to where Joe was lying. She swung the scope back to where Hector had disappeared from sight, just to see someone pop up. Slowly, she squeezed off another shot, hitting Pedro in the forearm just before he fired, causing his shot to go wide. He screamed with pain as the .55 grain bullet hit his forearm at nearly 4000 FPS, tearing apart the muscle and destroying bone.

Logan reached for Joe, grabbing him by the collar. He threw Joe over his shoulder into a fireman's carry, then he turned and ran back over the hill, dropping behind a dead tree for temporary safety as Kay and Rene both opened up, picking target after target. They kept the would-be human trafficking slime balls pinned down. With deadly accurate shot placement, one-by-one the gang of slime balls found themselves being ventilated and bleeding as the two women continued to give Logan cover fire.

Soon Joe and Logan started moving back towards the gold claim. Kay watched as Rene disappeared and reappeared, working her way towards where the guys had just disappeared only seconds before. Kay continued to find a few more targets of opportunity as she carefully scanned the area for slime balls that were still trying to get closer to where Logan and Joe headed.

Carefully, Kay slid backwards out of the two rocks she had been using as cover and slowly started working her way in the direction Logan and Joe had disappeared.

As she came around a corner, she could see Logan standing with his hands up. She watched as Santiago moved towards him with a pistol in his hand.

Kay slipped back, taking a deep breath and shouldering her rifle just as Rene walked in from the other side. She heard Santiago say, "Drop your gun and keep your hands where I can see them! Juan will pay dearly to get you. He's told us all that whoever captured you will be very well rewarded."

Kay slowly moved around the corner. Placing the cross hairs on the back of his head, she said, "Well it won't be you. Don't even think about it or the next person you'll be talking to, will be Satan. Just drop your gun before I blow your damn head off." Santiago had no choice. Slowly, he let his arm fall and his fingers released the pistol as it fell to the ground. "Now kick it towards the others. I'm done running from Hector and Juan and the rest of you. If you so much as twitch, I'll put a bullet in your skull. You'll be out of this forever. I have something I want him and that idiot Juan to hear. I want you to tell them. You have two choices. You either deliver my message or die right here and right now. So what's it going to be? Are you going to deliver a message?" Taking a deep breath, Kay looked around then back at Santiago. Continuing she said, "He has pushed us for the last time and you are going to deliver a message to him and that dumbass Juan. Now listen and listen well. If we so much as see any of you we'll start hunting and we will shoot to kill. So far we have all been just trying to wound, hoping you would get the message and leave us alone. That ends and it ends now."

Kay continued to slowly move forward towards Santiago. Sticking the barrel in his back, she pushed him forward. He slowly turned and gave Kay a look of pure loathing. That look pissed Kay off even worse as she kicked Santiago's pistol towards Rene. Santiago looked around and then from one to another of his captives. With a sneering scowl on his face, he said, "Hector wants you. He just takes what he wants and kills whoever is in the way."

Kay replied, "Well, I don't want him. He's nothing but a worthless piece of shit." Kay took three steps forward and kicked Santiago in the nuts, sending him doubled over to the ground. Looking down at him, she said, "Do you think you can remember what I just told you? Oh and make sure you tell him what I think of him. That he's nothing but a low life piece of human shit and not really worth the price of a bullet. Or maybe should I just put a bullet in your worthless ass and deliver your dead body to them? Or better yet, just leave your sorry ass here for the buzzards?"

Santiago closed his eyes and said, "Yes, I'll remember."

"Good," replied Kay, "now crawl back to that ass and tell him to either leave us alone or make his peace and to get ready to die."

With everyone watching Kay and Santiago, no one noticed as several of Hector's gang of slime balls walked in with. Kay had no choice but to lower her rifle. Rene stood stone still between Logan and Joe. She had both pistols in her hands and she put them behind her back. Carefully, she handed one to Logan and the other to Joe. Not knowing how many shots they had left was a problem. If they started a fire fight and ran out of ammunition first, the two guys would die. Probably very slowly and painfully. They would also be forced to watch as both Kay and Rene were raped in front of them.

Looking at Logan, Joe mouthed the words, "Attack or wait?"

Logan glanced at Joe and shrugged his shoulders. He had absolutely no idea what they should do. He knew that Juan would probably kill him and take Rene, but Juan wasn't there. He also noticed that Pablo was also missing. Maybe, just maybe, either Kay or Rene hit or possibly killed one or both. He himself had taken a few quick shots at them, although he wasn't sure he hadn't hit either. The shots were both hurried, just trying to give Joe cover fire when the attack began. He then noticed Joe was moving. He wasn't moving much, but like he was trying to get a better or more clear shot.

Just then Joe dropped to one knee and took four quick shots, killing the men in front of Hector. Kay's rifle cracked and another slime ball started to slide to hell. Logan's hand moved on its own. He felt the pistol jump twice as another was blown over backwards. Grabbing Kay, Joe called to Logan, "Come on, follow me."

Just as they made the exit, they ran smack into Juan and Pablo along with five more slime balls. Joe slid to a stop. Dropping his pistol, he slowly raised his hands. Kay stood her rifle against the rock wall and stood next to Joe. Logan pulled Rene behind him and let his pistol drop.

Pablo walked up to Joe and in broken English he said, "I'm a rich man. One million US dollars."

Joe looked at Pablo and said, "I wish I knew what you are talking about. Why do you keep saying I'm worth a million dollars?"

Pablo laughed and said, "Don't play stupid with me, Mr Ghost. You are not as good as everyone says. Look at you now. We won, you are going to Columbia. I'm going to get a million dollars. Plus Hector and Juan are getting your woman."

Joe whispered, "Don't spend that money yet. It's a long way to Columbia."

Pablo snapped around. "What did you say? Hey Juan, did you hear him?"

Juan stepped forward, reaching for Rene and said, "I didn't hear anything. Although I do want you." As he reached for Rene, Joe and Logan reacted at the same time. Logan's right fist made solid contact with Juan's jaw, snapping his head back and sending him crashing into the rock wall. Joe grabbed the guy nearest him. With an elbow strike to the man's throat, Joe had his M16 and opened up, killing the armed men first. While Pablo grabbed Juan, they ran for the safety of the nearby Jeep. Joe swung the rifle towards Pablo just as the bolt opened on an empty clip. With Joe out of ammunition, all they could do was watch as the two men ran.

Throwing the empty gun, he grabbed another and emptied the clip at the Jeep as it sped away. Looking at Logan, Joe said, "Let's get their weapons and try to get back to camp. Grab any and all ammunition they have."

As Joe and Logan went through the dead man's pockets, looking for anything that would help their fight and flight, Kay and Rene both grabbed rifles and watched for any sight that Hector was still around. Kay hooked the sling of her .22/250 over her shoulder. It was a gift from Joe when they had first gotten married and she had always loved the rifle.

When Joe had started shooting, Hector and three of his men all ran for cover. While at the same time Joe, Kay, Logan, and Rene ran in the opposite direction. As Kay and Rene stood guard, Joe and Logan finished. With everything being as ready as they could be, Joe led as he started working his way back to where they were camped.

Arriving back at their camp, Joe and Logan immediately started looking around, trying to see all the damage at one time. Broken windows, flat tires on the campers, and two pickups that looked like they had been on the losing end of a gun fight. There were windshields and side windows shot up too. Looking around, they found two rifles and walked to opposite sides. Kay and Rene headed into the campers to see what they could salvage out of the carnage and find what they could to make something to eat. Joe stood there thinking as he looked out into the desert for any sign of movement. Joe turned and watched as Logan walked across the camp. Stopping at his side he asked, "Do you think they are still around?"

Joe replied, "Absolutely, they are still here. Hector and Juan want the women and Pablo wants me. They'll try again. They know we are trapped and can't leave. It's a long walk to the highway and an even longer walk to where we can get help. Hey, do you have your phone? I asked Kay and she lost hers and so did I."

Logan quickly checked his pockets before saying, "Mine's gone. I'm not sure about Rene."

Kay came out of the camper just a few minutes after Rene. Both had made a few things to eat. Dishing up plates, they walked to their husbands. Kay glanced at her husband. There was something different.

He had changed into something she had never seen. Walking to his side, she asked, "Are you ok? There's something different about you. Something that scares me."

Joe shook his head. Putting his arm around her, he said, "I'm fine, just thinking. Then turning, he said, "I'm going to have you stay with Logan and Rene tonight. I'll help find a place where you'll be safe, then I'm going hunting. This time they went too far and someone…" he paused and stared out into the desert. Shaking his head, he again continued, "Hopefully all of them are going to die."

All four walked back towards the campers when Joe said, "Make a pot of coffee. Something tells me it's going to be a very long night. I'm sure they are not gone. We can't stay here and I'm going to be watching from the desert." Joe opened the door and went inside. Coming out a few minutes later he was dressed totally in black. Looking at Kay, he said, "Change your clothes. Put on all black if you can. Or the darkest clothes you have." Looking over at Logan, he watched as Logan took Rene's hand and said, "We'll be right back." They disappeared inside.

Twenty minutes later the sun sank into the western horizon and they all returned. Joe took a grease pencil and drew shadow lines on all exposed skin and said, "All the guns I could find are right here. Load up, make sure you take all the ammunition you can carry.

Kay swung a light backpack on and watched as Joe turned. A red laser dot tracked across his back and stopped. In one quick step, she knocked him to the ground just as a shot rang out and the bullet embedded itself in the camper.

Logan pulled Rene to the ground as he said, "Did that hit anyone?"

"No," Joe continued, "thanks to Kay, I'm okay."

Kay said, "I saw a red dot go across Joe's back and stop. I have a laser sight on a pistol Joe got me and knew what it was."

With everyone on the ground, Joe said, "That shot came from over there. Come on, follow me and crawl." He belly crawled under the camper and out into the desert.

There wasn't a moon and it was an absolutely black night. Joe continued to crawl until he saw a dark shape in a sea of darkness. Knowing it was a rock pile, he whispered, "Here's a rock pile. Let's get behind it."

Joe switched on a red shadow light, knowing it couldn't be seen more than just a few yards. He looked at Logan and said, "There's a small cave about twenty yards straight ahead. Take this and find it. All three of you get in there. I'll be back before sunrise." Kissing Kay, he whispered, "Always remember I love you." Handing the light to Logan, he continued, "Stay in that cave. They can't get in with someone back three to five feet. You'll have a clear killing field in front of you. They would have to blast you out and they can't get that close. Shoot anyone that can't answer a few basic questions." Knowing that no one would be coming to their rescue, he said, "The name of my horse. Cheyenne." With that, he kissed Kay one more time and belly crawled away.

Logan crawled the other direction with Rene and Kay following. In a few minutes he found the small cave. He went in first and checked to make sure there were no snakes or anything else that could bring harm. Crawling out, he said, "It's all clear. Get in there. I'll stay at the entrance and stand guard."

As Joe crawled away his mind drifted. Suddenly, he was in Iraq and there was a small Taliban patrol hiding just off the highway. They had planted a bomb in hopes of an American patrol coming past. He sat near the top of a low rise and watched as they placed the makeshift explosive in a shallow hole in the blacktopped highway. Covering the bomb with gravel, they walked a short distance up the mountain side and set up the ambush.

With darkness as a natural cover, the ghost made his way to within twenty feet of his target. He wanted to kill all except one. Letting one escape would only increase their fear of the night. Now ten feet away and moving only inches a minute, he continued towards the closest guard. Now only two feet away, he grabbed the guard, covering his mouth the 8 inch Ka-Bar slips between his ribs and killed him in seconds. Making no more noise than a snake, Randy slowly made his way from bed roll to bed roll, killing all except the last one. He slowly slipped away, leaving one alive to wake to the carnage the ghost caused in his late night visit.

Joe slipped across the desert and watched through his peripheral vision at movement. Slowly, he continued to crawl, making his way around so he came up from the rear. Now he could clearly see the guy watching the camp. He continued forward so he came up on the man's left side. Stopping, he watched as the guy played with his laser sight. Joe could see the red dots as it slowly moved across the camper. Inch by inch he moved forward. Now only a foot away, Joe reached up and pulled the guard over backwards with his hand over the man's mouth and his legs locked around the man's waist. Joe pushed the blade of his razor sharp hunting knife up through his lower jaw and back. Giving the blade a twist, he cut through his brain stem. The man quivered once and went limp. Joe quickly and quietly rolled him to the side and went out in search of another slime ball.

Crawling to the top of a rise, he laid there and quietly watched. Seeing movement again, below and slightly to his right, he started crawling. Before daylight, he was back at the cave and quietly called out, "Logan, Kay, can you hear me?"

Kay answered saying, "Logan, it's Joe. He's back! He's back!"

Kay crawled out of the cave and into the waiting arms of a tired and wet husband. Momentarily drawing back, Kay asked, "Why are you all wet?"

Joe replied, "I stopped at the pond and cleaned up. I got a little dirty tonight and didn't want you to see me that way."

Joe closed his eyes and said a silent prayer that his days of killing were coming to an end and that hopefully someday he'd never have to kill again.

Kay replied, "Dirty, bloody! As long as it's not your blood and you are okay, I don't care."

Joe crawled into the shade and pulled Kay close. In a few minutes while he was sleeping.

Kay slowly worked her way out of Joe's arms and told Logan, "Why don't you lay down and try and get some sleep. Rene and I will watch for a few hours. I'm sure by the time Joe wakes up he'll have some kind of a plan to talk with you about getting us out of here. Remember, we do have several ounces of gold in the mine."

Logan crawled a few feet as he said, "That sounds like a great idea." Rolling his light coat into a makeshift pillow, he was fast asleep in a few minutes.

A few hours later Joe suddenly jerked wide awake. Looking around for just a few seconds, the activity from his late night visit came back to him. He knew that Hector and his gang of slime balls would be just a little nervous for the next several nights. Especially when he had killed one guy and left the other alive only ten feet away.

Moving a few feet to where Kay and Rene fed small pieces of wood into a fire, he asked, "By any chance is the coffee somewhere close?"

Kay and Rene both jumped at the sound of his voice as they replied nearly at the same time, "I only wish."

Joe smiled and said, "As soon as Logan wakes up we are going back to the camp. After dark tonight we can use that flashlight I gave Logan and get one of the pickups drivable. That way we can get out of here and hopefully get some help. With just a little luck Hector won't have the police in this area on his payroll as well."

Logan stretched to his full six foot three inch length as he started waking up. Setting up, he looked around and asked, "Is Joe up?"

Rene crawled forward and kissed him. She replied, "Yes, like an hour ago. He wants to get one of the trucks drivable so we can try and get out of here."

Logan started getting to a standing position and said, "That's a fantastic idea," just as Joe and Kay walked up.

"What's a fantastic idea?" Joe asked.

Logan reached for Rene as he replied, "Getting a truck running and getting the hell out of here."

Just as the daylight faded into darkness, the four friends headed for the campers. Joe looked under the front of both and said, "This isn't going to work. I'm sure we won't be going very far. There are bullet holes in both radiators. Looks like we had better come up with a secondary plan. It's close to fifty miles to the nearest town."

While looking at the front of his truck, Logan said, "Maybe we can pinch off the tubes with enough damage to get there? Or at least part of the way."

Switching on the red light, Joe looked at the radiator in Logan's pickup. Then walking to his, Joe replied, "I think mine is hopeless. We might be able to cobble yours. It looks like there's about four holes in yours. Someone emptied a full magazine into mine. I didn't open the hood to see how much more damage there is."

Grabbing a tool box in a few minutes, they started. As the front of the pickup came apart, they just dropped the parts they removed to the ground. Knowing they would not be putting it back together, Joe took his hunting knife and carefully placed it between the cooling tubes, cutting the aluminum fins and giving him access to the tubes. With a pair of pliers, he squeezed the tubes off and tried to bend them over where he could. The outside core was easy to reach. It was the deeper tubes that gave him trouble. Logan walked around, looking at the tires and checking to see how many needed to be replaced. Logan smiled as he said, "We only have to change one. I don't think we need duels to get out of here."

It took them nearly two hours to get the pickup somewhat drivable. Joe looked at Kay and asked, "Get a bucket of water? Let's see how many leaks we have."

Carefully, he poured water into the radiator. Looking below, he saw a small trickle. Looking at Kay, he said "Grab all the water bottles we have. I think we might make it twenty miles. The way it is now. With a little luck, maybe more."

Joe watched as Logan walked around the end of the camper and said, "Get all the ammunition you can find, plus any guns they missed. I hope we don't have to fight our way out of here. I want you to drive with Kay and Rene inside with you. I'll ride in the box where I can shoot in any direction. Mostly straight back."

With the radiator full, they loaded up and prepared to leave. Logan, Rene, and Kay all climbed inside. Joe started to climb into the box when Kay said, "Oh, no! You get inside with us. I don't want you back there with nothing to hide behind."

Holding up his M16 he said, "I'll be hiding behind this and a curtain of hot flying lead if we get attacked again. We were able to get all of this done without them attacking tonight. I think my late night visit to their lookouts may have been enough to scare them."

Kay replied, "I don't care, Joe. I still don't want you back there with absolutely no cover. If they do attack you have nothing to get behind."

Looking around, Joe saw the stack of coolers next to the camper. Putting several in the box and a strap over them, they were ready to try. Kissing Kay one more time, he closed the door and climbed into the box. Picking up the rifle, he slipped in a full magazine and pulled the activator to load the chamber. Giving Logan a thumbs up, he dropped below the coolers as they headed out of the desert in search of help and safety.

Logan hit the starter and they headed for the road leading out of the desert. Watching the temperature gauge, everything went great for the first ten miles. When they came around a corner they saw a road block. Hector and his gang of slime balls had two Jeeps across the road.

Logan stopped about five hundred yards away and said, "Oh, shit. Now what?"

Joe stuck his head in the back window and said, "Hit the gas. Wide open. That heavy ranch bumper should offer a lot of protection. The rear of those jeeps are light. You should be able to ram your way through. I'll keep them either pinned down or running for cover."

Logan smashed the throttle to the floor. The rear of the truck fishtailed as they gained speed. Joe stayed low, hanging on and watching through the windshield as they accelerated at the roadblock. Just as one of the guys raised a rifle, Joe popped up over the cab and opened up, spraying a lethal curtain of death. As the slime balls first saw then heard the sound of a fully automatic rifle being fired at them by someone that knew how to control it. They felt hot lead and heard the sounds of bullets hitting all around them. Joe slipped in another magazine and opened up a second time. Then dropped and held on as the seventy five hundred pound pickup hit the two Jeeps at high speed. The heavy bummer does its job and held together while pushing the two light weight Jeeps out of the way. Joe spun around and leaned on the coolers. He opened up a third time spraying death and destruction as they sped down the road and out of sight.

Five minutes later Logan had no choice but to pull over because the temperature gauge was climbing. Stopping as they rounded a sharp turn in the road, Joe jumped out and ran back to where he could cover their back trail. Kay and Rene watched in front. Logan grabbed four gallon size jugs of water and started filling the radiator. Pausing, Logan could hear the sound of water trickling and saw two new leaks. Grabbing two branches from the roadside, he pushed them into the two bullet holes.

In the matter of a few minutes he hollered to Joe, "Hey, come on. Let's get the hell out of here!"

Joe sprinted back to the truck and jumped into the box as Kay and Rene climbed in. They were moving once again.

Arriving in a small country town, they had several things they needed to find. First they visited the local cell store and bought four new phones. They left them to be uploaded with all the information they have stored in the cloud. Next was a sporting goods store where they purchased more ammunition for the guns they still had.

Joe looked at Logan and asked, "Hey, are you hungry?"

Logan answered, "You know I haven't thought about food. But now that you mentioned it, absolutely." Looking down the street he continued, "There's a restaurant. Should we grab something quick?"

Joe looked around before he spoke, "No, let's just sit down and relax. If that ass is in the area there should be too many people around for him to do much."

With breakfast done, they enjoyed another cup of coffee and tried to come up with a plan to get headed for home when Logan noticed people walking past and looking in the windows. Kicking Joe's foot under the table, he nodded at the front door and windows. Joe slowly turned looking at the window as his hand slid inside his jacket and gripped the pistol. While his other hand grabs his wallet. Handing it to Kay he ordered, "Get up and pay the bill. I think we have company."

Kay's eyes opened wide as she started to shake while a few tears started to run down her face. Walking to the register, she handed the waitress a credit card as the waitress inquired, "What's wrong? Why are you crying? Was the food that bad?"

Kay wiped the tears away and explained, "No, the food was great. We are running from a known drug smuggler and human trafficker. They want the other lady and myself. Our husbands don't like that idea and we have been in several fights. I'm so scared that they will be killed. I can't take much more."

The waitress glanced at the window and asked, "Is it Hector Ortiz?"

Kay's eyes snapped to the waitress as she questioned, "Yes! Do you know him?"

"Yes," the waitress sighed, "he and his men come in here from time to time. They don't stay long. The law enforcement in this area have sworn to kill him on site. It's just he's not scared of them. In fact he's killed several then runs for the border. They can't follow him into Mexico, and the Mexican government doesn't seem to care."

Looking at the other waitress she whispered, "I'll be right back."

Turning to Kay she invited, "Come on, follow me."

Kay motioned to the others to follow as they walked past. Arriving at the back door Logan demanded, "Stop. Let me go first."

The waitress explained, "No, not outside, go through that door, it goes to the basement. There's a tunnel that connects several of these buildings together. They were built over a hundred years ago when there were still outlaws and Indian raids. The woman and children would either hide or run."

Joe felt the cold steel of a pistol on his neck. Freezing, he heard in Spanish, "Don't move, all I want is the two women."

Joe replied in perfect Spanish as he spun pushing the pistol to the side just as fire blossomed from the barrel. The bullet harmlessly embedding itself in the thick wooden walls. As his hand came out with his knife, Joe roared, "I don't care what you want."

He buried the knife in the man's side as he yelled, "Run!"

Down the stairs and into the tunnel, they all ran four buildings later they came up. Just a couple hundred feet from where the pickup was parked. Looking through the window, they then ran for the pickup and headed for the next town where the sheriff's office was located. The twenty mile trip took fifteen minutes, and the pickup was running hot as they came into town. Stopping as the engine finally gave up and quit. Exiting the picky they ran the last three hundred yards to safety.

EPILOGUE

Running into the sheriff's office, Joe took a quick look around. Spotting central dispatch, he yelled, "I'm Joe West. We could really use some help!"

Upon hearing the name Joe West, the duty officer jumped up, drew his side arm, and grabbed Joe by the jacket and ordered, "All you follow me now."

He took everyone down the hall and found a secure room. He directed everyone inside and closed and locked the door. He holstered his side arm and asked, "Can you please show me some identification?"

Joe slowly turned around a little nervously as he produced his driver's license with his right hand. His left was empty and close to the opening in his jacket. Kay, Logan, and Rene all produced their license as well. They all started asking questions and heard a knock on the door. The duty officer slowly opened the door with his hand clutching the pistol on his belt.

Another officer walked in and identified himself as Sheriff Dale Rogers. Looking from one to another he asked, "Which one of you is Joc West?"

Joe stepped forward with his left hand still close to the opening of his jacket. Sheriff Rogers requested, "Would you please come with me?"

Joe barked, "Sorry, but no! After everything that has happened, I'm staying close to my wife and not letting her out of my sight."

Dale looked at Joe with a look that told Joe he knew more than he was letting on. Finally he explained, "We have multiple APBs issued for you and your friends. I've been in close contact with the DEA in Tucson, mostly a man named Chance."

Joe looked at Kay and assured her, "It's ok. I'll be right back."

Following Dale, they exited the room and walked down the hall to his office. Once inside he closed and locked the door.

Turning he offered his hand and said, "It's an honor to meet you, Joe."

He pointed to a letter on his desk. Joe glanced at the letter and saw the name Randy Jackson.

Taking the offered hand, Joe smiled, "It's a pleasure to meet you also, Sheriff Rogers."

The sheriff replied, "Please call me Dale. Would you follow me?

With that the two men walked down the hall to yet another room. Closing the door Dale flipped on two switches on the wall and explained, "We can talk freely here. This room is soundproof plus I just turned on electronic jamming."

Joe replied, "I'm commander Randy Jackson, US military and undercover agent DEA retired. We have had several, shall I say

unpleasant problems with Hector and his friends. For some reason Hector thinks he should have Kay, and that idiot Juan wants Rene. It's gotten to the point that if I don't kill them both, they will kill Logan and myself and just take the women. We need help getting the hell out of here. I'll give you the GPS location of our gold claim. There you'll find my pickup, two campers plus a couple of ATV's all shot to shit from when they attacked us. If you search the area, you'll also find several dead bodies. If I see either of the two I just mentioned or a fat Mexican named Pablo you'll find three more. Pablo is with the Colombian cartels, and they want me some kind of bad. In fact there's a million dollar reward. From what I know and figured out, it must be alive. I don't believe it's a dead or alive contract or they would have killed me when they had the chance."

Dale scratched his head and said, "I'm sure we can get your belongings out of the desert and bring them here. Even though I know the story, I'll treat it as a crime site and keep it secured. I'll help you and your friends out of the area."

Joe replied, "Talk to the Tucson DEA; I'm sure they will help in most any way you ask. Although for tonight we really just need a safe place to stay with a hot shower, good food, but mostly safety."

Dale looked at Joe and said, "I can help with all of that plus tomorrow I'll personally bring you to the airport in Tucson so you can catch a flight home."

Joe smiled as he dropped into a chair. Taking a deep relaxing breath and saying, " Wow, thank you. You have know idea how much we will appreciate it."

Stepping back Dale Rogers snapped to attention and saluted Joe, "I didn't know you until today although your reputation arrived several years ago."

Together they walked back to the room with Logan, Rene, and Kay.

Opening the door a worried Kay ran across the room into the loving arms of her husband.

Joe unlocked and opened the door to their home, then reaching over he keyed in the six digit code to deactivate the alarm system. Carefully he walked through the house and checked all the rooms, turning lights on and off as he went. Arriving back in the living room he said, "It's all safe, hon. We are home safe and sound."

Taking the four guns they managed to bring home, Joe walked into his gun room and placed them on the bench. He walked back to the living room, opened the doors on the fireplace. In the matter of a few minutes he had a nice fire cracking.

Watching the fire for a few minutes he turned and walked into the kitchen. He watched as Kay went through the cupboards looking for something she could make for supper.

Kay looked at the single suitcase that carried both her and Joe's clothes home. As she was unpacking she folded everything making piles. Then looking at Joe she smiled saying," I think I'm going to have to go shopping. Nearly all of our clothes were in the camper."

Joe walked over wrapping his arms around her, "The camper, pickup and everything else is replaceable. All I needed to bring home was you."

Kissing her long and deep he continued, "You are the reason I live and breathe. You are the only one in my life that matters. The only one I can never replace."

Twenty five miles southwest of Tucson, Hector and his gang were about to cross the border back into Mexico when they were stopped by the DEA. As the officers approached the Jeep, Hector drew the stolen .45 H and K semi automatic pistol that he had taken from Joe. As he rolled down the window, he opened fire and Juan jumped out and fired at the second officer, killing the first officer. Slowly Hector opened the door and got out of the Jeep, limping, he slowly walked over to where the second officer lay bleeding. Looking down at him, he smiles, aims and pulls the trigger. Getting back in the Jeep, they turned south and crossed into Mexico.

Pablo says, "I can't believe you lost him. He is worth a lot of money."

Hector screamed, "I lost him! You were there. I didn't see you trying to find him at night."

Juan hollers, "Would you two shut the hell up? I need to think. We need to figure out a way to separate them. I want Rene."

To be continued…